Served with a Twist

Served with a Twist

A book of short stories

Ajay Garde

PARTRIDGE

A Penguin Random House Company

To order additional copies of this book, contact
Partridge India
000 800 10062 62
www.partridgepublishing.com/india
orders.india@partridgepublishing.com

Contents

ACKNOWLEDGEMENTS

This book is a result of constant encouragement over the past year, causing even a lazy person like me to take up writing seriously.

I thank my wife Anuja and my daughter Anoushka, for keeping me focused on my writing and believing in my effort.

Thanks to the set of my closest friends, whom I call, 'The Gauls' (Abhijit, Bharat, Dolreich, Gerard, Nachiket, Thomas, Sumit, Sameer, Samir, and Shailey) due to startling similarities in behaviour with some of those comic characters.

Also, thanks to the editors at Partridge for their assistance.

1

A Lesson in Moderation

I MET BILL FOR the first and last time in my life at a pub in the port city of Hull, on the eastern coast of England. The pub, called the Dog and the Bone, was adjacent to the bed and breakfast where I was staying for the night and, as per the receptionist of my B&B, was also a popular watering hole for sailors. I was taking a break from sailing and was on a sightseeing tour of England and Europe. When I entered the pub that Saturday evening, the place was already full of thirsty souls. Music could be barely heard over the continuous chattering of all those people. Searching around, I finally located an empty stool and had barely seated myself at the bar counter, when Bill threw a dart that bounced off the dartboard and pierced the back of my left hand. He came up to me and apologised profusely, as he plucked out the dart. The bartender quickly administered first aid, accompanied by a pint of bitter on the house.

After the game, Bill came up to me and suggested that we move to a table in the corner that had just been vacated. I agreed, as sitting on a backless bar stool had often caused my backache to return with a vengeance. He introduced himself and sat down in front of me with two pints of bitter, one of which he pushed towards me, as an offering of apology. After the truce, we got talking amicably. When he came to know that I was a Master Mariner, he was delighted and told me that he had been sailing as a chief officer and was presently on examination leave. Bill was a brown-eyed, red-head who stood about five feet six inches tall, weighed about forty-five kilos and was perhaps in his early fifties, almost ten years older than me.

It is common knowledge that whenever two sailors meet, the talk is only about ships and sharing experiences, both, at sea as well as in ports. This is just what we ended up talking about. It was obvious that he had been anchored in the pub for several hours, as he was showing the effects of having consumed sufficient alcohol to float a lifeboat in. He roared with laughter when I told him an anecdote about one of the voyages which had taken me to a remote tanker terminal outside a port somewhere in Venezuela in the early 90s, where I had seen a donkey that had been strategically placed, just outside the terminal gate, which was trained to take a passenger, straight to a brothel about two kilometres away. After we had exchanged a few similar stories, he was already treating me like an old friend.

'I am going to get drunk tonight, AJ,' said Bill. It seemed to me that he was on the right path, as he was clearly in the second half of his intention.

'Let me tell you the secret of life, mate,' he said, genially and then looking around to see that all was clear, whispered to me with slightly unfocused eyes, 'Moderation!'

I said that it was good to hear. His eyelids were now drooping from time to time, so I was sceptical about his claim but did not say so. If this kind of drinking was moderation, then Oxford's needed to review the meaning of the word. He must have guessed that I was merely being polite, and his eyes suddenly opened wide.

'You think I am joking?' he demanded, looking suspiciously at me and frowned. I immediately assured him that I was sure that he was sincere in his claim and that I believed in it as well.

'Well, mate, I will tell you all about it and then you shall judge for yourself, if I am telling you the truth. A more curious tale, I bet, you will never have heard,' he assured me, not satisfied that I was convinced.

'Back in 2001, I had been sailing on the Sea Crest, a small container feeder ship, on a regular basis, consecutively for the past six years. I had a back-to-back relief with another chief officer, every two months. Do you know why I kept going back on the same ship?' asked Bill owlishly. When I said that I had no clue, he said, 'I had a flourishing business going on there. Yes, sir. The Sea Crest had been on the same run for the past ten years, plying between Rotterdam, Antwerp, Aberdeen, Stavanger, and Hull. A round trip would take us two weeks, so it was quite hectic. The idea for the business came to me all of a sudden after my first round trip, in February of 1995. I was on my first shore leave at Stavanger in Norway, when I went to a local pub with my bosun. It was extremely cold, so I and the bosun knocked off a couple of shots of scotch and then almost got into a fight with the bartender. See, the cost of a single shot of scotch there was £8, which we didn't know at that time, and we had about six shots each. Can you imagine paying £96 for twelve shots of whiskey? Anyway, we paid up reluctantly, when the bartender threatened to call the police, and immediately left the bar. Seething inwardly with rage at such prices, it actually got me thinking. When we were on the voyage back to England, I did a few calculations. Since one standard shot of 25 ml cost £8, then a standard bottle of scotch would yield 700 ml and each bottle would hold twenty-eight shots, which meant that a bottle would cost £224!' said Bill, with excitement, almost as if he was reliving the exhilaration that he must have felt that day, eighteen years ago. As for me, I marvelled at the way this man's brain had worked out the calculation, despite his present state, having soaked himself in alcohol.

Bill drained his pint, motioning me to do the same, and called out to the bartender for two more.

'Anyway, where was I?' he asked, scratching his head. I repeated his last sentence, and Bill smiled and nodded as he recollected what he had been saying.

'Thash's right. Sssssorry. Ahem! So I got to thinking. Here was a golden opportunity for me to make some money, but it would need to involve a few people, if the venture was to be successful. I thought, if I could create a supply chain which involved key people, I could get a fantastic business going. And that's when I held a meeting with the bosun, second engineer and the cook. See? I had covered all the departments on board to avoid any conflicts! They all agreed and then there was no looking back!'

Bill was flushed with excitement as he said this. I looked around me to see if anyone else had been listening to his story. Luckily, all the people in the pub were busy with their own discussion and no one appeared to have taken the least bit of notice of his monologue. I was curious how Bill had managed the so-called business. It was clear that he had been involved in the illegal transportation of liquor into Norway, or what the Americans used to call 'boot-legging', back in Al Capone's time. But how had he managed to avoid the authorities, I asked him, since Norway had very strict procedures and policing in place, where alcohol was concerned. The bartender came up to us with two more pints and setting down the mugs in front of us, looked at me with a smile, and said, 'Congratulations, sir.'

I was a bit puzzled. He must have thought that I was someone else. As I was about to explain his error, Bill hastily waved away the bartender, as if he were a fly and immediately returned to where he had left off, immune to the dark look that he got from the bartender.

'AJ, let me tell you how I organised it all. That was a piece of cake actually. In the second voyage, I and the bosun picked up one bottle of scotch each, from Aberdeen, at £15 per bottle. When we reached Stavanger in Norway, I requested the local shipping agent to take me ashore and drop me near the fishing wharf, which was about two kilometres from our ship's berth. Earlier, I had convinced the captain that I had met a fisherman last time on shore leave, who had promised to sell me some fresh fish at a cheap rate. The agent, who had probably done this before, did not suspect anything and happily dropped me off at the fishing wharf, and upon my insistence that I would make my way back to the ship, he drove away. With me, concealed in my winter parka, I had two bottles of scotch. I proceeded to examine all the boats lying along the wharf. There was a lot of activity going on, and I had to search for a while before I found the boat I was looking for and its owner. Before sailing from Hull, I had contacted my cousin Vincent, who was a fisherman himself and owned a fishing trawler. From him, I had obtained the name of a trustworthy and discreet Norwegian fisherman. Of course, Cousin Vincent wanted a piece of the pie too, didn't he? Now this cousin of mine is actually related to me quite distantly, being the youngest son of my late Uncle Dick and his third mistress . . . 'I stopped Bill here and told him to forget Uncle Dick and his mistress and that he was drifting from the main story of his business.

'Of course! That's what I was telling you, wasn't I? Ha ha ha. How strange that I drifted off the topic. OK, so anyway, I met with the fisherman whom we had codenamed Thor and gave him both bottles as a token of our deal. We finalised the details of how each drop would be carried out, how it would be collected, who all would be in the loop, and how the money was to be paid. At the end of our deal, I bought some of the fish that he had caught that morning and walked back to the Sea Crest. Besides Thor and meself, nobody had a clue what arrangements had been decided. It was simple actually. I, the second engineer, bosun, and the cook would buy twelve bottles of different scotch each, at Aberdeen during our shore leave, and store it in the steering gear room. The bosun would make four parcels of twelve bottles each in a waterproof garbage bag and lash it with a strong fishing line. He would then secure a white polystyrene float to each of the parcels. These were then stowed inside some rusty old steel pipes from the engine room which were lashed on the poop deck for God knows how many years. During passage from Aberdeen to Stavanger, we would always pass east of Storvokjor Island. Since our ship's schedule always placed us around this position between 6 p.m. and 7 p.m., I would always be on my bridge watch. I would use the aldis lamp to flash a Morse signal, 'Bravo' three times in the direction of the mainland where Thor, who would be in his fishing boat off the coast, would flash back, 'Charlie', which meant all clear or, 'Foxtrot' if there was danger. I would then relay this to the bosun. He and the Cook would drop the parcels overboard from the stern. Thor would then retrieve the parcels with a boat hook and take them to the mainland, covering the booze with his day's catch of fish. Thor would then sell the bottles to a man he knew, who owned a pub. Payment would be made to him on the spot, and there was never any problem. Thor would then wait for one of us to go down to the fishing wharf, which would normally be the cook, to collect the money and buy some of his fresh fish, just to ward off any suspicion from curious eyes.'

He stopped to gulp down half a pint, and putting the mug down, he wiped his mouth with the back of his hand.

'So that's how the business took off. We had always been discreet with our trade. We always shared all the proceeds between the ten of us, without anyone getting upset with his share. Meself, my relieving mate, the bosun and his reliever, the second engineer and his reliever, the cook and his reliever, and of course, Thor and my cousin, got along fabulously with this arrangement for six years! Except for November, December, January, and February, we would carry on with this trade for the remaining eight months. In those six years, I made roughly £20,000 per year, tax-free. But then in September 2001, everything went haywire, courtesy of Osama Bin Laden,' Bill said mournfully, lost in his own thoughts. After a minute of silent reverie, he shook himself out of his stupor and emptied the beer mug in one go. I was still on my second beer and my third one was still untouched. He looked at it wistfully. I merely pushed it across to him, and he gave me a grateful look.

'How was Osama Bin Laden responsible for your business to go bust?' I asked, now curious where the story was leading. I could see no connection whatsoever, since, according to all reports, Osama must have been a teetotaller.

'AJ, be patient, and you will hear the best sermon on moderation from me,' said Bill as he took a gigantic sip of his umpteenth beer.

'As I said, our business had flourished into a fixed trade. We were never greedy, and everyone was happy. That August in 2001, a new Master joined our vessel in Hull. Captain Higgins was his name. He was a brute of a man, six feet six inches tall, powerfully built, and extremely nosy. He somehow found out about our little trade by the time we had sailed from Stavanger and confronted me. He demanded to be included in our deal, or else he would put a spanner in our entire works. I had no choice but to agree with him, and upon reaching Hull, I immediately informed Cousin Vincent and all the others except Thor, as he did not have a phone. Captain Higgins was a bully and sneered at me in contempt when I told him that we stuck to forty-eight bottles for each deal. When I, the bosun, second engineer, and the cook were summoned to his cabin a few hours before arriving at Aberdeen, we were uneasy. Onboard, the three of us would never interact socially. Just so that no one would have any suspicion. I remember that when I had told Cousin Vincent in Hull, he had been furious. We had even contemplated aborting the trade temporarily.'

I waited patiently until he had drained his pint. Without asking, I hailed the bartender and held up two fingers and pointed at our empty mugs. Bill grinned at me for being a sport. He had now reached the stage where an interlude, such as this, caused his eyes to shut automatically and he would nod off to sleep. Thinking that he had had enough, I was about to tell the bartender to cancel our orders, just as he thumped down the two pints in front of us. There was hardly a sound of the mugs banging on the table in the noisy pub, but to Bill, it must have sounded like an atom bomb. His eyes flipped open instantly, and he grabbed the nearest pint. I was amazed at such acute hearing prowess.

'Well, what happened next?' I asked eagerly. I had to know how Osama Bin Laden was responsible for Bill to start believing in moderation.

'Huh? What was that?' asked Bill, appearing confused at my question. I patiently explained what he had told me so far and saw cognizance returning to his eyes.

'Ah! Yes, Captain Higgins. The bastard! May hell roast his soul!' cried Bill with agitation and shook a fist in the air, in anger. He took a deep pull at his beer, which seemed to calm him down somewhat.

'Captain Higgins called us to his cabin, a few hours before we were to arrive at Aberdeen. He told us that he did not believe in making peanuts from such a trade. He wanted the whole tree. He told us to go and buy not twelve bottles, but six cases each! Do you know what that means?' Bill hissed with his teeth clenched. I said I did. Each case contained 12 bottles, twenty-four cases would contain 288 bottles. Bill nodded.

'He told us that he would take care of the transportation and the security man at the terminal gate. All that we four had to do was go ashore at Aberdeen, meet his van which would be waiting for us outside the gate, drive around town, and pick up two cases from twelve different liquor shops each. We protested that the exposure to risk during the entire gambit would be too high. Also, Thor would not be able to pick up all the stuff by himself. Where and how would he sell this much of booze and that too without notice? No, we said, the plan was too rash and unplanned. Captain Higgins roared at us. I think he would have assaulted us had we not agreed with his plan. In hindsight, I think the plan would have worked,' said Bill thoughtfully.

'So it did not work,' I concluded. It was nearing 10 p.m., and I had to wake up early to catch the train to Manchester. Bill muttered something, deep in thought, and took another huge sip of beer before continuing.

'Of course, it didn't work, did it? We got the stuff on board, and the cook put it all away in the provisions store. There were a lot of comments by the crew and officers, about how much food was coming on board, but surprisingly, no one took it further, as the crates were all marked 'Soy Sauce' or 'Ketchup' or 'Vinegar' on the sides. That was Captain Higgins's idea. He had also told us when we were in his cabin that he would stop engines just near Storvokjor Island for testing main engines in all modes, including safety trips and emergency stops. This would give us chance to signal Thor, wait for his boat to come alongside, and dump all the stuff straight into his boat. Although the plan was a good one, we four were a bit uneasy.'

'Anyway, we sailed from Aberdeen, terrified as well as eager to make a solid profit this time. Exactly as planned, Captain Higgins adjusted the ETA to our drop-off point to 7 p.m., 11 September 2001. We arrived off Storvokjor Island in complete darkness and had slowed down. Two radar targets could be seen, one to our north and one to our south-east, both about six nautical miles off. I was on the bridge with Captain Higgins who had the con, when we were hailed on VHF Ch. 16 and ordered to stop immediately. I noticed that both the targets had increased speed and were approaching us at 20 knots. Captain Higgins swore loudly and told me to run down, get the others, and dump all the crates overboard. With trembling legs, I ran down to the poop deck and found the bosun, second engineer, and the cook already there. I blurted out what had happened, and they stood frozen with shock. Just then, a powerful searchlight was directed at us. It was the Danish Navy destroyer, astern of us on our starboard quarter. Our engines were now stopped, and we were drifting. There was nothing we could do to cover our tracks now. It was too late to throw out our crates. Anyway, we were boarded by the Danish and Norwegian Navy chaps, who ransacked the entire ship and found our booze. To cut a long story short, the ship was arrested and anchored inside Stavanger harbour, with six armed Navy fellows on board. It seems, New York had been attacked by planes flown by terrorists a few hours earlier, and there was a red alert for any suspicious aircraft, ship, or persons all over Europe. It was just our bad luck that Captain Higgins had slowed down to make the drop off just then. Had we stuck to our original plan, I think we would have escaped without problems. Or if Osama had not carried out those attacks on that day, we may have made a whopper of a profit. Anyway,

I ended up spending five years in prison. Two for the illegal booze in a Norwegian prison and three in the custody of some really nasty people, who wanted to see if we had any connection with the terrorists.'

I was astounded hearing Bill's story. So that's why he blamed Osama Bin Laden and was all for moderation. Sighting that both our mugs were empty, Bill said, 'AJ, how about one for the road?'

I agreed and suggested that we have a scotch on the rocks to wind up our evening.

'Make it a double then,' pleaded Bill.

I ordered the drinks, just as the bartender was about to ring the bell for last orders, and got them back to our table, where Bill had once again nodded off to sleep, his head resting on the crook of his arm on the table. He had now started snoring lustily.

I put the two glasses down. The moment he heard the glasses touching the table, he woke up instantly and grabbed the glass closest to him, a remarkable feat to do, when one is snoring in decibels liable to cause legal action for noise pollution.

'Here's to your good health!' he exclaimed and downed the contents at one go.

I returned the salute and took a sip. I excused myself to head for the washroom just as he put his empty glass down. When I returned to the table a few minutes later, Bill was nowhere in sight. I waited for a while, and when he finally did not show up, I went up to the bartender.

'Do you know where Bill is?' I asked him, a bit concerned. He looked at me with a puzzled stare.

'You know the guy who was sitting with me, the same fellow, whose dart hit me earlier this evening?'

He shook his head and said he had not seen him. I was confused. I looked around amongst the crowd of revellers to see if I could spot him. A man sitting on a bar stool, next to where I was standing, suddenly spoke up.

'Here, mate, are you talking about the guy who was sitting with you?'

'Yes, sir, that's right. His name is Bill. Do you know where he went?'

'Bob, you mean.'

'No, no. His name was Bill.'

The man shook his head impatiently and clucked his tongue to correct me.

'That was Bob, not Bill.'

Puzzled at this, I continued, 'Anyway, do you know where he is?'

The man laughed out loudly and shook from side to side, holding on to the bar.

'Say, that's funny! I thought you and he were thick. Did he say his name was Bill?'

'Yeah, but that still doesn't answer my question, mate,' I said, slightly miffed at the man's behaviour.

'Sorry. Ha ha ha. Looks like 'e has pulled a fast one on you, hasn't he?'

'What the hell are you talking about?' I said angrily.

'Well, the last time I remember seeing him at another pub, he was called Bob.'

I looked at the bartender who had been listening to our conversation quietly. Seeing the question in my eyes, he said, 'He told me that he was waiting for a friend when he came in at five this evening. Since you two appeared to be friends, I thought he had been waiting for you.'

'How many rounds did he pay for?' I asked, in a daze.

'None. He told me to put it on the tab and you would settle it all at the end. He said that you had had a lucky break in some hush-hush business up in Norway and were coming here to celebrate with him. That's why I congratulated you earlier. He said that both of you had sailed together on some ship called the *Sea Crest* where you were the captain.'

Furious with this piece of information, I quickly ran towards the door to see if I could catch up with Bill or Bob or whatever he was called, before he could escape. The bartender and the man on the bar stool followed me. Looking around in the night, we could see nobody resembling Bill. Dejected, we headed back into the pub. I had been had.

'Well, bartender, how much do I owe you?' I asked fearfully.

The bartender looked at me in embarrassment.

'Look, sir. I run a straight business, and this kind of behaviour will give my pub a bad name. Tell you what, we will split the bill, least I can do for you.'

'Why! That's really kind of you, mate. Thanks. So how much do I have to pay?'

'Your half comes to £150, sir,' said the bartender, consulting a scrap of paper.

I had nothing to say, so I paid up, and wishing the bartender a good evening, I went back to my bed and breakfast.

Since the episode with Bill, I have always been on guard whenever I hear the word 'moderation' and avoid going to church when the sermon is likely to be on the same topic.

2

The Changing Wind

THE SMALL VILLAGE of Parasgaon was situated at the foothills of the Sahyadri range, in Satara district of Maharashtra, in India. The people of this village like many others similar to it, within a radius of a few kilometres, had remained neglected by the government since 1947 and continued to sustain their existence through menial labour in the fields and farms surrounding the village. No change had taken place in this region since Indian Independence. Even the NH-4 national highway was almost fifty kilometres away. Rain too was an infrequent visitor to this area in monsoons, due to a unique natural curvature in the mountain range which caused rain clouds to be isolated from this area. Although all villages boasted of a village panchayat, there was hardly any external influence to improve governance.

It was 1995 and the state government had decided to introduce electricity in all villages in Maharashtra. Coal prices had become exorbitant, and the cost involved in setting up a coal-fired electrical generation plant was seen to be too expensive. After several proposals and schemes suggested by genuine developers, as well as the regular scamsters, the government decided to appoint any legitimate company which was renowned for providing power generation facilities through wind farming. The necessary tenders were demanded and scrutinised. Finally, a reputed international company was selected. The project in India was to be headed by Arvind Belkar, an experienced forty-five-year-old mechanical engineer who had worked around the world on similar projects for the company. As with any new project, ground realities were required to be sounded and resolved. This had been handled by Belkar and his deputy Vikas Mhatre, a civil engineer. Vikas had spent one month on preparing the project report, visiting the villages and surrounding areas, with Belkar. To set up a wind turbine, it is essential that the speed of wind is almost constant. This was not the case in the areas they had scouted so far, mostly on foot. At last, they located a place on top of a hill range where the average wind was found to be consistently in the range of 25-30 kilometres per hour. Ideally, the turbines should be situated at least 30 feet above any obstacles, and at least 300 feet surrounding the turbines should be clear. The place they had found was better than perfect.

The village panchayats had initially received these newcomers with suspicion. Gradually, when they learnt what the project would involve, they had become enthusiastic. Electric power was only something which they had heard of, while some had experienced it during their rare visit to the cities. As the land on which the wind-turbines would be constructed was on top of a mountain range, the land belonged to the government. So at least the company did not have a problem with land acquisition. In the first meeting with the sarpanchs or heads of the village panchayats of the nineteen villages who would benefit from the project, a briefing was held by the project's chief engineer. In layman's terms, he explained how wind would cause the turbine fans to rotate and how this would in turn generate electricity. The enthusiastic support from the panchayats was evident when they started shouting slogans, glorifying Belkar's name. To them, electricity meant progress, and progress meant schools and hospitals and most importantly, employment opportunities.

Soon thereafter, a site office was set up at the base of the proposed hill range close to Parasgaon. Work had now started in full force, and reels of high-voltage cables and equipment were being delivered at the site office almost every day by trucks, after leaving the highway and moving onto tiny meandering dirt lanes. Enthusiastic villagers sent their team of workforce for assistance. There had been a meeting of the village heads from each of the nineteen villages earlier, during which they had decided to provide assistance to the company for completing the work faster. Each village panchayat head had deputed a team from his village which took turns at digging from Monday to Saturday. This improved manpower was a blessing to the project's chief engineer. As most of the electrical cables were to be run through underground piping, starting from the top of the mountain to its base, this work was left to the villagers. The deputy project manager, Mhatre, directed his team of six company employees and the teams from the villages to the correct places for digging. It was in the third week after the work commenced that the first hiccup occurred in the project. An ex-MLA from Satara visited the site office on the seventeenth day after the project had started. Four white SUVs with ex-MLA Ganpatrao Raut and a bunch of his followers drove to the site office at around 3 p.m., amidst clouds of dust. As the doors of the SUVs opened and slammed shut, the chief engineer, with his site supervisor Shinde, was in his small site office, going over the inventory of PVC piping and high-voltage cables that had arrived. The on-site security guard Mohiuddin knocked on the cabin door.

'Come in!' said Belkar. Mohiuddin entered and stood to attention. He was an ex-military man and still had the same ethics and mannerisms expected of a soldier.

'Sir, there is a man called Ganpatrao Raut outside who is requesting to see you,' said Mohiuddin. The chief looked perplexed. He had no idea who the man was.

'What does he want?' asked the chief.

'No idea, sir. All he said was that he would be obliged to meet you,' replied Mohiuddin.

'Is he alone, or is anyone else with him?' inquired Belkar.

'He has about twenty people with him waiting near their cars. Two men are with him in the waiting room, and the rest are just hanging around outside,' replied Mohiuddin.

'OK, send him in. Alone. Shinde, don't leave. We still have to discuss the inventory,' said Belkar to his site supervisor. Mohiuddin saluted and went out. After a minute, there was a knock on Belkar's door.

'Come in,' said Belkar. The door opened, and a short, thin man with a salt-and-pepper beard, dressed in a white kurta-pyjama, walked in. The man appeared to be in his mid-forties. A jagged scar running from his left ear all the way to the corner of his lips was faintly visible through his beard. A dark blue scarf was wound around his neck. From the movement and colour of his mouth, he appeared to be chewing tobacco. The man stood in the doorway with both palms together and a smile on his face.

'Namaste, sahib!' said the man softly and bowed. 'I am Ganpatrao Raut. I am a social worker in this area. I just wanted to pay my humble respects to you.'

Belkar looked at the man and nodded. 'Have a seat, Mr Raut. What can I do for you?' he queried, a little mystified. Raut sat down in the chair opposite Belkar.

'Sir, firstly I wanted to thank you for bringing such a fantastic project to this part of the country which has been left neglected since Independence. You see, we were neither considered to be in Konkan nor in any part of the industrial or agricultural belt of Maharashtra, hence unworthy of government attention to development. My grandfather was part of the freedom movement and would have been extremely pleased to see such a great project starting in this neglected area,' said Raut in a humble tone.

'Thank you for the kind words. But it is the government that you should be thanking. Under the central government scheme, all the rural areas in the country are to be electrified. This project is just a part of it. In fact, this is one of the first projects,' said Belkar.

'I am truly happy, sir,' said Raut, smiling as he chewed on his tobacco. Belkar looked at Raut, wondering where this was leading to.

'Look, Mr Raut, if that is all, then I request you to forgive me for asking you to leave, as I am in the middle of some important work,' said Belkar. Raut's smile slipped momentarily and then came back on again.

'Sir, please allow me to present my case. You see, as a social worker, it is my job to ensure that all people get fair treatment. I have been led to believe that you are employing villagers from nineteen villages in the vicinity which will get electricity, for doing menial labour on this project. Now I have no objection to people working, but I have been informed that they are not being paid for this work of digging. These are poor and simple uneducated folk, sir. Now I am not judging you personally, but I do think it is unfair of your company, a reputed and rich international company, to take advantage of these poor people. Hence, it is my request to you to hand over the money to me in advance so that I can distribute it amongst them,' said Raut softly, with a humble smile. Belkar showed his annoyance with his tightly pursed lips and a frown on his face.

'Mr Raut, I am not sure where you have got this information from, but please let me assure you that it was the panchayats of all these villages who insisted on sending their team of work-hands for speeding up the project. We already have our people working in the field. I had clearly stated to the village panchayat heads that we would not be able to pay the village teams. You can understand that we work on budgets approved by the company, so I am in no position to pay the villagers. If the villagers expected to be paid, then they should have come to me or discussed it first with their village heads. I fail to see any reason why I should pay you!' retorted a visibly upset Belkar.

'Come, come, sir. Please do not get angry. I am merely stating what I had heard earlier and just now, seen with my own eyes. Look, to ease your worries, I am prepared to accept 25 lakh rupees (2.5 million rupees) on their behalf for ensuring that the work does not get delayed. If not, there may be no villagers coming to assist you in getting the project completed on or before time,' said Raut in his cool manner, still with the gentle smile on his face.

Belkar got up and walked around the table to where Raut was seated.

'Look, Mr Raut, I will only say this once. I will *not* pay any money to you. If the villagers want money, they can forget about it. I don't care if they do not come for work. I will still complete the project with my people. I know what you are. A bloody hooligan! Don't try to take me on, Raut, I have worked all over the world and seen enough nasty people but still managed a 100 per cent success rate. You want the money for yourself and are just putting the villagers into it as a means to getting your hands on the cash. Get out and stay out! I do not want to see you again, understand?' shouted Belkar. Shinde stood rooted to his place, his face white as chalk. He had never seen the chief engineer this angry, and this was a sight he was not prepared for.

Raut sat unmoved throughout the tirade, the smile still intact on his face. He sighed, got up slowly from his chair, and said softly, 'Sir, I have humbly tried to convince you to see what is right. You are a big man working for a big company, and I respect you for that. However, it is evident to me that you will not agree to meet my terms. Well, at least not yet. So be it.'

Raut sighed shaking his head woefully, bowed with folded hands, and turned around towards the door. Just as he was about to exit, he looked back at Belkar with a mournful smile.

'Sir, let me advise you before I leave your office that your project will never be completed nor will it be operational. I may not have travelled the world, but I know people. I know the intricacies of how their minds work. I hope you will still be able to scrap up whatever remains of your reputation and dignity when this project is folded up,' said Raut and turned to walk out.

Belkar was shaking with anger. He followed Raut into the corridor and shouted angrily, 'You dare to threaten me? I will see to it that I and the project survive! The project will open on 25 May, exactly six months from today! Do what you want. You will not be able to alter the winds of change.'

Raut walked on without looking back, smiled, and softly muttered to himself, 'Winds of change. Now that is indeed melodramatic!' His two henchmen got up immediately when they saw Raut and followed him to their SUV. In a whirlwind of dust, the four SUVs left the site office.

Belkar was fuming when he returned to his office. A cowering Shinde stood in the corner, as if the boss was likely to assault him.

'Get me the commissioner of police, Satara. *N*ow,' barked Belkar. Shinde awkwardly ran to the list of contacts posted on one of the office walls, picked out the number, and dialled from the satellite phone.

'Good afternoon. I am Shinde. I am calling from Parasgaon where we have a windmill project going on. The chief engineer of the project, Mr Belkar, would like to speak with the commissioner. It is urgent. Thank you.' Turning to Belkar, he said, 'Sir, the commissioner is on line.'

'Good afternoon, commissioner. Thank you for taking my call. I wanted to make an official complaint against one Ganpatrao Raut, who claimed to be a social service representative for this region. He has barged into my office today and demanded 25 lakh rupees (2.5 million rupees) or if we don't give it, he will shut us down. I request you to provide police protection to this project,' said Belkar patiently. His anger had subsided now, but his hands still shook in the aftermath of the adrenalin rush.

'Raut? That guy is a troublemaker. Of course, I have heard of the project that is going on near Parasgaon and really appreciate what the government is doing. Do not worry, Mr Belkar, I will dispatch a squad of police personnel to keep watch on your project. In fact, I have been briefed by the home minister himself to provide any assistance to you should you ever require it. Rest assured. I will personally come tomorrow morning with my squad and discuss security issues with you,' said the commissioner in a soothing voice.

'Thank you, commissioner. By the way, who is this Raut?' asked Belkar.

'Raut is an ex-MLA. He is nothing but a mobster. But beware, he is not one of the regular cut-throat kind of goons. He almost never resorts to violence. He is the kind of guy who plays mind tricks. He is a well-educated man. Has an LLB and masters in psychology. If you don't mind me giving you a suggestion, pay up. Just pay up and forget about it. This man is one clever fox,' said the commissioner.

Belkar felt irritated with the way the commissioner was trying to play the whole thing down. Or was he trying to escape from his responsibility? Was it possible that the commissioner would get a cut from that money demanded by Raut? Should he call the home minister directly? Belkar was confused and impatient.

'Commissioner, I will do no such thing. I am not going to allow a hooligan to threaten or derail my project. I hope that you will provide me with the security as promised. I intend to continue doing my job without interference and finish the project on time. Hope to see you in the morning tomorrow, say around ten o'clock?' asked Belkar.

'Sounds fine to me,' said the commissioner, sighing unhappily.

*   *   *

As the procession of four SUVs left the site office, Govind Shirke, a lieutenant of Raut, spoke up.

'Dada, what happened in there?'

Raut smiled and told him. He knew that he was surrounded by fools and dim-witted hard cases. Only Shirke had shown the occasional flash of intelligence during the past several years. This had led to Shirke being appointed as boss-man, to rule over the remaining hooligans. They would have been shocked had they found out what Raut actually thought of them. Their devotion to Raut was beyond belief. After all, they had only rarely been required to beat up someone. Raut had the magic touch of not getting them into trouble, but still come out on top, victorious, like a prize-fighter who could knockout the opponent without laying a single punch.

'Govinda, what do I always tell you about anger?' asked Raut with his signature smile in place.

'Dada, you always say that the man who shows anger openly is nothing better than an animal,' replied Shirke. He had always been in awe of Raut. This thin and short man had saved him once from being arrested for the attempted murder of a liquor shop owner, who had refused to pay 'protection money' to him, when he was leader of his own band of hooligans. Not only had he gotten off scot-free, but the liquor store owner had eventually paid up the amount and even distributed free booze to him and his men, after Raut had gone alone to talk to him in his house. Since that time, he had acknowledged Raut to be his master and would gladly do whatever his master asked of him.

'So how do you think we will get the money? What should we do next?' asked Raut.

'Give me the order, Dada, and I will take a truck load of our men and break both legs of that chief engineer,' said Shirke hotly.

Raut smiled and responded mockingly, 'A truck load of men to break two legs of one man? Are you sure that this will definitely get us the money?'

'Of course, it will! If he does not agree even after that, we will threaten to burn him alive!' replied Shirke.

'And what if he still refuses? I don't think Belkar likes to lose,' queried Raut, toying with him.

'Then I say we burn the fellow in front of his colleagues. That will get that company thinking!' said Shirke proudly, as if he had suddenly discovered the way to nirvana.

'Don't you think they will send in the CBI to find out why the project is being stalled? Don't you think that we may then be targets of every law enforcement agency in the country? Do you think we will still be able to get our hands on the money? Don't you think that by now Belkar must have already notified the police of our little visit to him? Think!' Raut said with a frown. Shirke was suddenly nervous. He had seldom, if ever, seen his boss without the ever-lasting smile. Now he longed to see his master smile at him. He thought for a while before replying.

'Then let us threaten the villagers and tell them to back off the project, or else we will burn their village down,' said Shirke hopefully. Raut shook his head gently and smiled.

'You are lucky that you have me to look after you. God knows what would happen to you and the others if I was not there to guide you,' said Raut.

'Dada, just say the word and we will do it. You know that we will do anything for you,' said Shirke humbly.

Raut sat quietly, lost in thought as the procession of SUVs bumped over the dusty, un-tarred roads. After a few minutes, he said, 'We will pay a visit during the next all-panchayat meeting which is next week, discreetly. Just to see what their plan is. You and two of your men will accompany me but will say and do nothing. Tell the others to keep their mouths shut. You will ensure that any accusations or abuses thrown at you all, or myself, are to be taken with your heads down, in complete humble supplication. No one will raise their heads or look up. I will alone speak. Do you understand?' asked Raut.

'Yes, Dada. I will make sure to brief all the boys,' said Shirke, relieved to see the smile back on Raut's face.

*   *   *

The following day, the commissioner arrived at the site office at 10.30 a.m. in his official white Ambassador with the red light on top, which was followed by a large police van. He made his way to Belkar's office with two of his Sten gun toting police constables by his side. Mohiuddin saluted him and led the way, ushering him into the project manager's office, while the two guards stood outside the doorway at attention.

'Good morning, sir. I am Belkar, the chief engineer and manager of this project. Please take a seat. This is Mhatre, the assistant project manager, and this is Shinde, the site supervisor,' said a bleary-eyed Belkar, as he shook hands with the commissioner of police. 'Thank you for coming all this way to meet me. Sorry, I did not realise that it was such a long journey for you, but I am not too familiar with these parts. May I offer you a cup of tea and biscuits?' asked a much-relieved Belkar. He had barely slept the previous night as he kept thinking about the conversation with Raut which irritated and angered him as he ended up tossing and turning in bed, fuming all night. The commissioner acknowledged and sat down in the chair opposite after removing his peak cap and placing it on the desk in front of him.

'Tea sounds fine, Belkar sahib,' said the commissioner. He asked Shinde to send in the tea and sat down.

'Let us get down to business. I am here with a force of twenty police commandos waiting outside for instructions, under the able command of Inspector Damle. Please tell me everything about what happened. I also need a map of your project boundaries and all plans. Let me assure you that we will do everything we can to avoid any mischief through physical efforts by Raut. But trust me, this man is not the average goon-on-the-street. He does not just have a Master's in Psychology. He actually uses what he has learnt and adds his own stuff to it. He has never been implicated in any case since his name first surfaced as a possible criminal. We know for sure that he is a criminal, but he is too smart to get caught. The only reason that he is not in politics anymore is because he tried to take over the party leadership using his devious means. He was even asked by several opposition parties to join them. Curiously, he declined all offers by stating that he counted party loyalty supreme and since then he has been a political pariah. Now he owns and runs a truck company which keeps him legitimate. That is why I suggested that you give up what he is demanding and carry on with your project. You will see that you end up saving at least twice that amount when the project is completed, if not more,' said the commissioner in a tired voice.

Belkar looked sharply at the commissioner. This was not what he had expected a police commissioner to say. He decided to tread carefully. After all, he had experienced some very nasty people in rural Nigeria when he was setting up a wind farm there a few years ago. He had successfully out-manoeuvred the corrupt police and local hoodlums, and managed to complete his work in the given time.

'Sir, I am not one to give up. I have faced local opposition for projects many times in my career, and I have been at this job for fifteen years. I have been threatened with execution in Southern Philippines, kidnapped twice in Indonesia, and have even been beaten up several times in various African countries, when I refused to pay any so-called protection money. What makes you think that Raut is a special case?' asked Belkar.

The commissioner sighed and scratched his chin as he shook his head with a woeful look.

'Belkar sahib, you may have faced physical hardships everywhere else in the world but still managed to survive and execute the project. Not in this case. Do you know what Raut goes after? He goes after the thing which is most coveted and treasured by you. In your case, it is apparent that your pride in work and successful record of project completion are the things most affecting you. Well, he just loves that kind of a challenge. And I am sad to say, he has a 100 per cent success rate in whatever devious enterprise he undertakes,' said the commissioner.

'Sir, I too have a 100 per cent success rate in my projects, and I am unwilling to compromise on my principles. So let us stop looking for avenues which do not exist. I will have my assistant hand over copies of all the documents that you asked for to your inspector,' replied Belkar, now even more determined to see his way through. The tea arrived, and Belkar instructed Shinde to organise the required documents. As they sat sipping tea in the relatively warm cabin which had a table fan running on a generator, Belkar asked, 'What do you think will be his next move? If, as you say he does not resort to violence, will he try to stop the trucks from bringing in the equipment?'

The commissioner sighed and put his cup down.

'That's too obvious, but possible. We will try and cover that aspect as well. The trucks, I mean. Now tell me what was spoken between you both,' said the commissioner. As Belkar explained, the commissioner made notes in a small black notebook which he had taken out from his top pocket. After an hour, the debriefing was complete and both sat back in their chairs.

'OK. This is what I am going to do. The police commandos will secure your work areas. They will work in two teams, each on a twelve-hour shift. They have already got tents and equipment which they will set up nearby, at strategic locations. I will be in touch with Inspector Damle on the police wireless set every twelve hours. He will be in charge of the security here. He is assisted by Sub-Inspector Kishore. I will let Inspector Damle explain his security protocols to you and your team. You and a few of your team will be given walkie-talkies for keeping in touch with the security. I hope this meets with your satisfaction.'

'Thanks, commissioner. You have been very helpful. I am sure I will be able to complete my work on time,' said a relieved Belkar and shook hands as the commissioner got up to leave. Belkar escorted him up to his car from which a smart young cop in inspector's uniform with a name tag of A. S. Damle got down to open the door. The commissioner introduced them formally and requested Belkar to stay on while he briefed the inspector in his presence.

That evening inspectors Damle and Kishore briefed Belkar and his core team of five and Mohiuddin the guard, on security procedures that would be employed. The police commandos had pitched their tents within 100 metres of the work site periphery. Team 1 would take the security watch from noon to midnight under Sub-Inspector Kishore, and Team 2 would take the midnight to noon watch under Inspector Damle. Walkie-talkies were handed over to Belkar, Mhatre, Shinde, Mohiuddin, and one of the three Foremen who looked after the labour force, for communicating with them. The routines started immediately, and for the next few months, work went along at full swing with the villagers' continued support and without disturbance from Raut.

In the last week, during which the final testing and commissioning of the windmills project was to take place, all the panchayats from the nineteen villages came together at Parasgaon for a celebration. Belkar and his core team members and Inspector Damle were also invited. The commissioner of Satara had declined to come, as he was engaged in arranging security for a minister's visit to Satara. A wooden stage had been erected over which hung a gaudy pink canopy. Small paper flags in a riot of colours were hung all around the village square on thin ropes tied to branches of trees. A drummer and an ektara player sang songs in praise of God outside the village temple close by, under the shade of a banyan tree. People of the village mingled with each other, dressed in their finest. The heads of the panchayats sat on the podium on makeshift wooden benches which were covered with white sheets. Food was being prepared in a small tent nearby, from where women scurried back and forth with pails of water from the village well and utensils filled with food. It was around 5 p.m., and the sun was still high in the summer sky. Dry gusts of wind blew small dust devils across the fields in the distance, towards the hills on which the newly erected nineteen wind turbines, stood majestically. At the base of the hills stood a large white structure with a dark blue slanting roof which housed the generator and main electrical switchboards. In spite of the 43°C heat, the villagers showed so much vigour, as if electrified by the magic of the windmills. Belkar, his team, and the inspector arrived in a red SUV. The excitement in the air soon got to them as they got down. Almost at the same time, all the villagers and the panchayat heads committee stopped their activities, stood up, and started clapping and cheering. The chief sarpanch came down from the podium with two other men. He garlanded Belkar, his men, and the inspector and hugged each one of them. There were smiles and good wishes exchanged. They were then led to the podium by the chief and served water in steel glasses. The villagers sat down in front of the podium, some under the canopy and others under the surrounding trees. The chief raised his hands for silence and then picked up the loudhailer from the table in front of him. 'Friends! The day when we can call our villages modern is very near. As promised, the esteemed Belkar Sahib is close to completing the job of providing us with electricity. For this, I bow down to him humbly,' said the head of the panchayats, bowing to Belkar with folded hands which set the crowd raising slogans for Belkar's long life. 'We people of the nineteen villages have never been to school. But, I am sure that once electricity comes to our villages, we will have schools, hospitals, roads, and maybe even running water in our homes. I now call upon Belkar sahib to say a few words, before we begin the evening of festivities.'

Belkar got up amidst loud cheering and clapping from the villagers. As he made his way towards the loudhailer, the sound of two vehicles moving at high speed was heard approaching towards the assembly. In the distance, dust rose up as two white SUVs approached the gathering over the bumpy roads. All those gathered turned to look at this new sound, while some stood up to see for themselves.

Belkar's heart missed a beat, and he looked towards Inspector Damle. Damle immediately read the frantic look on Belkar's face and understood that the newcomers must be Raut and his men. He got up and eased his side arm from its holster. The entire party of panchayat heads started talking among themselves, curious about the two SUVs. The vehicles stopped about thirty feet from the edge of the crowd, which had now all risen to its feet. Raut got down from the first vehicle followed by five of his men. He bowed to the assembly and raised his right hand which held a loudhailer.

'My brothers and sisters, I request just two minutes of your time, and I will be gone. What I have to say is urgent and only for the good of this and the other eighteen villages,' said Raut.

'Silence!' roared the chief of the sarpanchs, from the dais. 'How dare you come into our village! You are nothing but a troublemaker. We know how you tried to get money out of Belkar sahib using our good names. Get out and stay out of our villages, or as God is my witness, I will have you dragged by your feet and thrown out,' shouted the chief, now red with anger, his large white moustache bristling with rage. The crowd of villagers had also started talking and making angry threatening noises. For a villager who has no material possessions to lose, his only pride is in his humility and his good name. They knew of the dirty trick that Raut had tried to pull on Belkar, using them as the reason.

It all happened suddenly. No one could recall later, who started it, but the first stone missed Raut and hit the windshield of one of the SUVs, shattering the glass to smithereens. An angry growl from the crowds preceded the shower of stones, which were hurled by villagers of all ages. Herd mentality is such a thing that the meekest will become a lion, and this is just what was unfolding. Inspector Damle snatched the loudhailer from the chief's hands and tried to pacify the villagers and stop them. This only seemed to infuriate the crowds even further, and soon, a steady hail of rocks was flying towards Raut and his men. Belkar and the others on the podium were frozen with shock.

'Stop, please stop, my brothers and sisters! I am here only to apologise to you and help you. Please hear me out,' cried out Raut, who now had several gashes on his head where some of the flying projectiles had found their mark. After five minutes of bedlam, Inspector Damle took out his service revolver and fired three shots into the air. The sudden sharp explosions took everyone by surprise, and as suddenly as it had started, the attack on Raut and his men stopped.

'If anyone tries to throw a single stone, I will shoot first and ask questions later,' snarled Damle over the loudhailer. As if waking from a trance, the crowd snapped out of their blood-lust.

Meanwhile, Raut had collapsed where he had been standing earlier, bleeding profusely from several injuries all over his body. The white kurta-pyjama was now dyed reddish brown, from his blood mixed with the dust. His five henchmen were relatively unhurt, having taken cover behind one of the SUVs. At a sign from Raut, they ran forward and lifted him, carrying him to the second SUV. Both vehicles were badly damaged. Raut and his party immediately took off, and then there was silence. The festivities were broken up as the mood was now repentant, for the average villager is normally a docile person and rarely throws tantrums of this sort. Belkar informed the panchayats that he and his team were returning to the work site immediately, as Raut could still be in the vicinity. He asked the chief to be present for the opening ceremony scheduled for the next day which was 25 May, with as many people from all nineteen villages, as possible, for witnessing the start-up of the generators. Belkar and team departed immediately.

In the SUV, the doctor that Shirke had brought with him as instructed earlier by Raut was cleaning and dressing Raut's wounds. Worried to the core, a shaken Shirke asked, 'Dada, are you all right?'

Raut took a while to answer which alarmed his henchmen. As soon as the doctor had finished his work on Raut's injuries, Raut told Shirke to stop the vehicle and put the doctor in the other SUV. This little effort caused fresh blood to ooze out from some of his injuries. As soon as the doctor was put in the other SUV, Raut sat up and grimaced.

'Relax, Dada. Get some rest. I really cannot understand why you did not want us to retaliate. We could have wiped out the entire gathering! One tiny little fire would have finished the whole village and all those people, in spite of that cop with the gun! Why, Dada? Why?' cried the distressed and impatient Shirke.

Looking at Shirke with his un-bandaged eye, he asked softly, 'Do you know what scares simple people the most, Govind?'

A mystified Shirke shook his head. 'It's the mere sight of blood,' said Raut quietly. 'A little blood, shed in the cause of your belief can produce results which otherwise would be impossible. Blood and injuries, both cause human nature to feel sympathy, no matter who is the injured party. Now instead of a simple city person, if it was a village simpleton who saw this, the results are tenfold. The average villager mourns his ill deeds much more than a city dweller and will go to great lengths to repent. Today marks the beginning of our victory march. We will now make ten times more money than what we had asked for from Belkar'.

Shirke looked away, convinced that Raut had lost his wits after the severe injuries to his head.

'Govinda, get ready for the next phase of our plan,' said Raut sharply. As he explained the next phase, Shirke's eyes grew wide with wonder. 'What a brilliant man his master was,' thought Shirke.

At 3 p.m. on 25 May, a huge crowd from all nineteen villages gathered at the site of the generator shed where the opening ceremony was scheduled to be held. Never before had so many villagers gathered at one spot. Many of them did not even know each other, being from different villages. A huge canopy had been erected for the villagers to take shelter from the merciless midsummer sun. The auspicious time of 4 p.m. was awaited eagerly, and the excitement was almost visible in the air. Belkar, his team, and Inspector Damle with six of his commandos waited impatiently for the minister of State for Power Resources to arrive with the police commissioner of Satara for lighting a holy lamp, breaking the traditional coconut at the site which would give God's blessings to the completed project and the formal ribbon-cutting ceremony. Of the few people who were invited to this remote area, there were a few journalists as well, to cover the story, and had arrived an hour earlier. After forty-five minutes, a convoy of cars finally made their approach towards the congregation. All the twenty commandos originally meant for guarding the facility were now engaged in providing protection to the minister, as he got down from his car. He was followed closely by the commissioner, as journalists immediately started clicking pictures. They proceeded towards the dais erected near the generator room, amidst clapping and drum beats. The minister shook hands with Belkar and his team and hugged the chief of the panchayats council.

At 4 p.m. sharp, the holy light was lit and the coconut was broken. Belkar signalled to one of his team to standby to release the main switch for the electro-hydraulic locks on all the nineteen wind-turbines, which was located in another small room near the main switchboard. Once the electro-hydraulic locks were removed, the windmills would start to rotate freely. It was just the matter of a minute. 'One little snip and all these votes are mine,' thought the minister in glee. Just as he was about to cut the ribbon, a loud shout was heard from the other side of the generator room. Everyone became quiet, wondering what was going on. Amidst the silence, Ganpatrao Raut walked up from one side of the generator room, one hand holding a loudhailer while the other held a crutch. His heavily bandaged head, arms, and legs, the crutches, and his forlorn aura were heart-wrenching for even the hard-hearted. The sorry figure stopped and raised the loudhailer to his mouth.

'Brothers and sisters, I have escaped from the hospital that I was kept in, to come before you once more in spite of my severe injuries, to tell you what I have found out.'

The minister's bodyguards and the police commandos started moving towards Raut but were held back by the chief of the panchayats council, with a sharp command and said, 'Let him speak.'

'You have all been betrayed! I have just found out from my sources that this is a plan for ruining your livelihoods!' shouted Raut.

'Here! What are you talking about?' yelled the angry and alarmed, red-faced minister. Turning to the chief of the panchayats and the commissioner, he asked, 'Who is this madman? Get him out of here at once!'

The commissioner stood frozen in his spot. This was what he had been dreading. A live circus, in front of the media. The journalists were busily clicking away on their cameras, while others watched the drama unfolding in front of them.

'Ha . . . ha . . . ha . . . ha. Minister sahib! It is no wonder that you expected these poor ignorant villagers to be thrilled by your so-called generosity and give you their votes in the elections next month. There! You have just given the game away, minister,' laughed the mocking Raut, as he saw the minister squirming and about to start protesting his innocence. The media people were very aware that this was an epic scene they were witnessing.

'My dear brothers and sisters, just hear me out before you decide to stone me to death. You can all see the state that I am already in. In fact, I am here alone. Why would I lie? Just hear me out, please. Do you know what these windmills are for? No, not even one of you knows the real reason. Listen, you have heard of '*fans*'. What do fans do? They blow air away from them. This is exactly what these windmills are designed to do. They are going to blow all the monsoon clouds away from your villages! Clouds which should be bringing you rain for your crops! All blown away towards Sutarwadi, the hamlet where this esteemed minister and his many friends have acres and acres of farmlands! What will happen? You will be dancing and rejoicing for the electricity that you think you will get, but your fields will suffer! This is the truth, my brothers and sisters, I have no cause to lie. Think! What would I gain from this?' said a visibly tired Raut, who suddenly appeared to be a prophet to all the villagers who were watching and hearing him now.

The growl from the enraged crowd took Belkar by surprise. The minister had already started back tracking his footsteps towards his car. While Belkar appeared bewildered, the minister appeared to envisage his immediate future, and the commissioner just groaned in defeat. The villagers went berserk. So, they had been taken for a ride by all these people. Well, they were not taking this lying down.

While some villagers attacked the generator room, others made for the distant windmills themselves, tearing down everything in their way while Belkar and his team watched in helpless stupefaction as the crowds demolished every standing structure. The utter chaos and mayhem which followed was unbelievable. The police commandos sheltered the minister from the hail of stones and bricks, as he ran for the safety of his car, followed closely on his heels by the commissioner. The convoy with the minister, commissioner and all the commandos disappeared within seconds. Earlier that day, the commissioner and his senior inspectors had been sternly told by the minister that their primary duty was to provide security to him at all times. Within minutes, the peaceful festivities had turned into a chaotic battlefield. Belkar and his team ran for cover to their office. The media having filmed the fantastic turn of events rushed towards their vehicles as fast as they could, so as to put their news on primetime TV. The only person standing without moving a muscle was Raut, watching the destruction in fascination and satisfaction, and in spite of all the bandages, with his signature crooked smile in place.

After two hours of violence, the villagers left all the nineteen windmills, generator room, and other equipment in complete ruins, weary but satisfied, clouds of dust blowing all over the remains. It had taken more than six months for the project to be completed, but merely two hours to destroy everything. Belkar came out of his hiding place in a daze and looked at the ruins in agony. His team was still cowering inside, licking their wounds which some of the flying stones had caused. It was 6.30 p.m. and the sun was still devoting its remaining energy to light up the northern hemisphere. The dusk, heat, silence, and dust created an eerie atmosphere. He walked up to the ruins of the generator room and sighed with tears in his eyes. His body trembled in the aftermath of the unbelievable violence that he had just witnessed. Raut, now sitting on the ruined platform, looked at Belkar without expression. Belkar looked at him with unseeing, tear-filled eyes.

'Why?' whispered Belkar. 'What did you gain out of this destruction? Don't you realise that now neither of us has won? *Why*? Answer me!' screamed the infuriated Belkar. Raut looked at him steadily without expression.

Some of his wounds had opened up and had started bleeding again, reddening the white bandages.

'I had warned you, Belkar sahib, that in the end, I always win. Would it not have been easier to just hand over the money that I had asked for initially? Still, you cannot claim that I did not warn you,' said Raut as he rose up to leave, dusting his backside with his one good hand. He turned and limped towards where he had parked his SUV, behind some trees near what had once been the generator room.

'But . . . but what did you gain out of all this!' cried out Belkar.

Raut stopped, turned around, and smiled sadly at the mournful Belkar and said softly, 'A little more than just the winds of change, Belkar sahib, just a little more than the winds of change.' And he walked on into the evening mist.

The next day dawned to greet an empty landscape at the site where once the nineteen windmills had stood in all their majesty. Not a single piece of the huge windmills, cables, or generators could be found. This caused an uproar and the state government immediately set up an inquiry panel to ascertain what exactly had happened in the incident at Parasgaon. Opposition parties demanded the immediate resignation of the government. Local police investigation into the disappearance of all the expensive equipment produced no hard evidence, except rumours that on the night of the episode, villagers had heard several large vehicles coming and going from the site and had thought that trucks from the windmill company were coming to salvage what was left of their equipment. The central government handed over the case to the CBI as millions of dollars' worth of property was involved. There was a hint of suspicion that somehow, Raut had been involved in the disappearance of the equipment. The CBI team could not get any hard evidence against him, as his alibi showed that he had spent that entire night in the general ward of the government hospital at Satara, recovering from his wounds. Each and every single one of his trucks was searched thoroughly. Curiously, all of them were parked outside Raut's godown, where they were normally parked and were absolutely, spotlessly clean.

It was several weeks later that Raut walked out of hospital with a slight limp. The rear door of the white SUV with dark-tinted windows opened, and he got in and sighed. He had pulled it off, just as he had planned. He had made a deal with his contacts on the black market when he had first seen the starting of the windmill project. The day when the villagers had destroyed everything, few of his men had gone in hired trucks that night to sweep up the damaged windmills, generators, and cables. The workforce was huge, so they had got it done before 3 a.m. From there to the Konkan coast was just two hours' drive, where everything was transferred from the trucks to the waiting trawlers. They had further ferried the goods to a cargo ship, drifting offshore in deeper waters. From there, the ship had sailed to an unknown destination. He had made millions in profit of which he would pay a tiny fraction to his team of gangsters, but even that amount was staggering. As he sat back with his crooked smile in place, he wondered what he would have done had Belkar accepted his first offer.

3

The Journey

THE PAIN HAD started more than a year ago. After several tests were done at the General Hospital, he had been diagnosed with terminal cancer of the colon. Derek Fletcher was stumped. He decided to get a second opinion, so he went along to a reputed Harley street doctor who confirmed the previous findings and added the more depressing news that he had just six months to live. He called his three sons that afternoon and told them to meet him in the evening at the old-age home where he had been living for the past year. When he broke the bad news to them, Fletcher could see the light of greed in their eyes when they thought of the insurance money that would come to them once he was gone. That was when he had felt himself going deeper into depression.

Until the age of sixty, he had lived a life of constant struggles and hardships; he had been robbed of all his savings, his mortgaged house had been confiscated, and his stake in the company stolen by his business partner. He was too old to make a fresh start, so he entered into a home for the elderly in London. He could not bear to think of the humiliation he would suffer if he stayed at the dilapidated flats of any one of his sons. In any case, he doubted that he would be welcome. The small amount of money that he had kept aside for emergency was the only thing that remained. Just a few months before he had been ruined, he had started getting shooting pain in his stomach. As he had already gotten his appendix removed when he was younger, he was alarmed. Still, he had waited until the pain had become unbearable and so after two months, he decided to go to a doctor.

His entire life had been one filled with more hardships than normally handed out by fate to any common man. He had lost his parents when he was but three years old in an accident. Then the next twelve years had been spent at an orphanage in Falmouth, in the south-west part of England. Prospective parents who came for adoption had looked at him and turned away, almost as if on intention. Or perhaps it was just a play of fate which was against him. At fifteen, he had completed his elementary school education and then decided to take the option of going for work during the day at the docks and earn some money for night school. He left the orphanage when he reached sixteen. He had to struggle for five years before he ended up with a diploma and a decent job as a shipping agents junior clerk. The following year, he had met Lucy Perkins, a saucy and voluptuous barmaid with the face of an angel, who worked at the pub that Fletcher used to frequent every evening for his pint of ale. Within six months, they had married, and three years later, he was the father of three boys. He thought that he had at least gotten an encounter with happiness, although fleeting. Lucy had run away with his boss's son after two more years had passed, so Fletcher, who was by then a senior clerk, decided to quit his job to avoid the humiliating talk that he knew went on behind his back.

He had left Falmouth and had made his way across to London, along with his three children in tow. There, he had put in all his savings and set up his own shipping agency. He had taken on a partner to share the large investment and had also taken a substantial loan for a house. His kids were looked after first by a part-time nanny who had given up within a few months due to their malicious and devilish nature. He had felt guilty about raising the boys without any supervision and always thought that their bad behaviour was an outcome of missing their mother, although he never scolded or beat them, out of this guilt. When they were finally old enough to fend for themselves and sent to school, his eldest son had been caught trying to sell drugs. After he was expelled, the younger siblings had taken over his mantle and were likewise thrown out of school. Over the next few years, Fletcher had to bail them out of prison several times. Then, they had gotten involved with an organised gang and had finally left his house not by their own choice, but that of the constabulary, without bail. When they finally got out of prison, they went their own way and forgot all about their father. He had continued to send money regularly to all three of his sons just so that they did not go hungry, never realising that the money was not spent the way he thought it was. Drugs, women, and gambling were the only things that his sons were passionate about and spent on whenever they were out of prison. Working steadily, honestly, and earnestly over thirty years, he had managed to reach a point where things had finally started looking better for him, until his partner had stolen everything from him.

It was on a cold Monday evening in January that he was hospitalised. The doctors had given him six months at the most, and he had survived double that time so he knew that he was on borrowed time. The duty warden at the old-age home had called the ambulance immediately when he saw Fletcher doubled up in agony on the common TV room floor late that afternoon. After he was admitted to the hospital, the doctor on call had immediately summoned the next of kin. All three sons had taken their own time to come over. After sitting by his bedside for some time, they had appeared so eager to see him die that Fletcher told them to leave him alone. The ungrateful creatures had left immediately. The cold weather and dark skies outside were depressing enough, but the howling wind which brought an onslaught of snow made it even more gloomy that even the heating in the hospital could not take away. He had already made his will and had handed it over to his lawyer, a man he had been friends with since childhood. In any case, he had almost nothing to pass on. As he dozed on the hospital bed with various monitors connected to his body, listening to the typical hospital sounds such as the squeak from an un-lubricated wheel of a stretcher being wheeled past his door, the sharp and alert sounding footsteps of the doctors on duty, hastening from one patient to another, and the occasional bout of coughing from a fellow inmate from the adjoining room, he felt a presence in his room. He opened his eyes suddenly and looked at the far corner near the door. Alarmed at what he saw, he got up so suddenly that pain shot through the left side of his stomach, and he groaned in agony, as beads of sweat collected on his forehead. He saw a figure covered from head to toe in a dark maroon robe with no visible face, carrying a long-handled scythe. All he saw under the cowl were what appeared to be, two red pinpoints of light.

'Relaaaax. Don't be frightened, my friend. I mean you no harm,' said the figure, in a slow deep voice that curiously ended in a chuckle. A strange stale smell filled the room.

'You . . . y . . . you . . . wh . . . who . . . are . . . you?' stammered Fletcher, his voice trembling with fear.

'Sorry, I don't carry my business cards around. Well, not when I am making personal calls anyway,' said the figure from the corner sarcastically and guffawed. 'I am sure you know who I am, Mr Fletcher, and what I do. Haven't you been waiting for me these past twelve months? I regret I was so busy in Afghanistan, Iraq, and Syria that I just could not find the time to attend to you. You humans don't realise how difficult it is to multitask in my profession. There is just no time left to pick up the scheduled regulars,' said the figure in the corner in a forlorn and tired voice.

'Are you crazy? I don't know who you are and what you are doing here, and I don't want to know. Just get out, *now!*' shouted the now terrified Fletcher, wondering what the figure in front of him was ranting about.

'Shhhh, quiet! Come, come. We must not get so upset, OK? I am only here to do my duty. I am after all the Grim Reaper,' he said calmly.

Shocked into speechlessness, Fletcher sighed and lay back on his pillow. Tears flowed from his eyes. This wasn't how he had imagined his life would end. All alone, with no loved one around.

'I know it all, Mr Fletcher. You have certainly had a rough time, eh? Still, you think things couldn't have been worse?' queried the Reaper shaking his head.

'I don't understand. Why are you picking on me? I knew I was dying and was actually looking forward to it. But, I have struggled all my entire life, and I have never done anything wrong knowingly. I have lost everything that I worked for and yet, now I am going to hell!' said Fletcher, bitterly. The Reaper peered at him for a long time and chuckled.

'Now look. I am only here to pick you up and send you on your way. That's all. Decision making is not in my work portfolio,' said the Reaper and shook with mirth at his own humour. Fletcher glared at the Reaper. This was just too much. After all his hardships, losses, and now in constant agony due to the pain in his side caused by the cancer feasting away on his intestines, this apparition from the devil had the gall to joke about his miseries with visible glee as he was being taken to hell!

'Come, come. Let us not go with bitterness. You must come to terms with the future,' said the apparition, reading his mind.

'What future, you ghoul? You stand there in that corner with that big scythe in your hand and tell me that I have a future? Is there something seriously wrong with you?' shouted Fletcher in anger.

'Hush . . . save your breath, Mr Fletcher. We don't want to be interrupted during such an important occasion, do we? You see, should anyone drop in here and see me, I would be obligated to carry him or her too. The problem is that I have come here only in my two-seater. Arranging logistics, you see, is also not part of my job profile,' the ghoul guffawed.

'You are sick!' spat out Fletcher. He felt disgusted with this 'Thing' in front of him. Bitterly he told himself that he would resign to his fate. What choice did he have anyway? Life had not been kind to him, and he had assumed that death would be kinder. 'Well,' he thought tiredly, 'it now looked like even that was also unlikely.' He closed his eyes and took a deep breath.

'Look, you are not going to sleep, are you? It's just that I have never had a chance to chat up with a customer for a very long time. On your part, it is not polite to drop off to sleep when someone is talking,' said the Reaper, chuckling again.

'I am not going to listen to any more of your nonsense. You do what you have to and make it quick!' came the sharp retort from the bed, his eyes blazing open with anger.

'Do not get so angry and stressed, my friend. It's bad for the heart and blood pressure. You want to get a stroke?' said the Reaper, cackling softly at his own wit.

'Look, I am just doing my job. And I confess that I like humour. It just makes my job that much more pleasant. You think I like my job? You should see some of the customers I have to deal with. So attached to life! They have had their life's worth of happiness but still insist on getting some more. Is there no end to it? Did they come into this world with a pre-signed certificate that they shall live forever? I ask you! C'mon, Mr Fletcher, you know how it is. When humans are born, they come into this world with an unprinted, undisclosed expiry date. No one beats the system. Can you imagine if the seven billion people inhabiting this world today were given an endless life? Chaos! Utter chaos would be rampant! The seven billion would keep reproducing, and in no time, you would be double or triple that figure. I am here to maintain that balance. Of course like I said earlier, I only take away without being responsible for deciding who, where, and how,' said the Reaper now looking serious. 'It is time, my friend. We should be on our way. The journey is not long, but I do have more appointments to keep. As I said earlier, I am already late by a few months. Think of this as extra time as they do in football,' said the ghoul, laughing at his own joke. Fletcher sighed. He knew that he had no choice in the matter. He had done what he had done with his life. Now that death was literally on his head, he decided to let go peacefully. He took a final look at the corner and saw that the Grim Reaper understood his readiness as Fletcher closed his eyes for the last time.

When he opened his eyes, he saw in front of him what looked like a tunnel made of dark swirling clouds. The Grim Reaper was at his side holding his hand while they floated into the tunnel of the grey-black clouds, like that of a hurricane, from the centre of which a bright light seemed to be radiating. There was no up or down, left or right, and Fletcher realised with amazement that the pain in his stomach had disappeared.

'I am already dead, right?' he asked the Reaper.

'Yes, my friend. It was not as painful as you thought it would be, was it?' queried the Reaper.

'No. Did you chop off my head or something with that scythe?' asked Fletcher, eyeing the scythe while looking for traces of blood on its sharp edges. The Reaper appeared deeply embarrassed.

'No, Derek. I will let you into a secret. You see, at the beginning of time when I was given a wide option on my uniform, I decided on this cloak, and this scythe as my tool of trade. I have never used it to cut anything, not even a blade of grass. It is just a tool to go with my uniform. Others in my business use swords, tridents, or other fancy apparatus. I thought that with the title of Grim Reaper, this outfit would perfectly fit my job profile. You see, there were very few applicants for this job, so when we took up this work, we were given concession on the outfit and work name. The Grim Reaper sounds terrifying, does it not? It was actually just my humour going overboard. I did not realise how badly it would affect people. I immediately applied for a change of work-name, trade tool, and uniform. However, the higher ups were extremely pleased with my performance and decided that just one look at me, or even the mention of my name, actually assisted the client in releasing his or her soul more readily. Hence, I am now stuck in this predicament,' said the Reaper in a strangely deep and woeful voice. 'Popularity does have its downfalls too,' he sniggered heartily.

'So how long have you been on this job?' Fletcher queried. All fear, anger, and anxiety had left him. Strangely, he felt completely peaceful. That still did not mean that he trusted the ghoul standing next to him.

'Since the beginning of what you know as time,' said the Reaper.

'Well, now, I have a few questions.'

'Go ahead. I don't promise to answer what I don't know,' said the Reaper.

'Is there really a God?' he queried. The Reaper looked at him sharply.

'That's a funny question to ask, Derek. You have been listed as a believer. Tell me that I am not wrong,' said the Reaper in a worried voice.

Fletcher frowned. 'You can't answer a question with a question. Just tell me if God exists or not. A simple yes or no will suffice.'

The Reaper appeared deep in thought. He seemed to mutter something under his breath which curiously sounded like foul language.

'Yes. God does exist. Otherwise, we all wouldn't be here,' said the Reaper.

'What does he look like?' asked Fletcher. Reaper sighed, now exasperated.

'He looks like everyone and everything. He is everywhere and all over.'

'Then doesn't he weigh good deeds against bad deeds before he decides to drop anyone into hell? Is there no ounce of ethical rationalism?' demanded Fletcher bitterly.

The Reaper sounding more exasperated exclaimed, 'Hey! I don't know how he works. He just commands and that's all. We just follow his orders. Ethics, you know is not a word that I am allowed to familiarise with. It's you humans who make your rules for your own selfish ends. I do not know and neither do I want to know how and why. I just maintain my silence. As you would have noticed, I don't speak much and neither am I allowed to,' he said seriously. There was a period of silence as Fletcher digested this piece of incredible information.

'How do you know when and who to, as you said, pick up?'

The Reaper whistled softly and said, 'Until now, all the questions that you have asked me have been asked before but no one has asked me that ever. Anyway, here is how it goes. I believe that it is to do with the balance of good and bad souls and that too not just on earth. I or one of my colleagues get notified by the Superior to proceed for a pick up from a certain location. Once we get there, we track the person whose soul appears to be loose from his or her body. That's where it gets complicated as there is scope for making mistakes by picking up the wrong one if they are near each other. You see almost all people whose souls are loose give out similar signals whether the soul is good or bad. Unfortunately, callous as it may sound, we have to live with that. But it all gets balanced out eventually. And just so that you know, it is something the Superiors are presently working on but haven't perfected yet. I did come around once to pick you up twenty years ago, but at the last moment wars broke out somewhere in the world which made the Superiors change their plans. You see, finally all bosses are alike. Change their orders at the slightest whim. No idea how tiring it is to travel around continuously,' the Reaper chortled at his own jest.

'OK. Although I am not too happy about getting picked up just to be dumped in hell, what criteria do you have for deciding who goes to heaven or hell?' inquired Fletcher, again touching on the same topic.

'Hey, like I said earlier, I don't make the decisions on who goes where. Apparently, I am not qualified enough,' said the Reaper bitterly, but immediately moderated his voice. 'Although, I do sincerely feel sorry for you. Last question, please?'

'Exactly how bad is hell?' he asked, with fear lurking in his eyes. The Reaper snickered with delight.

'Wait and see, my friend,' he said while appearing to do a jig.

'No. You have had all the fun so far. I want to know just how bad things are going to be.'

'What do you imagine hell is like?' asked the Reaper seriously, the two red glowing eyes peering through the cowl at him.

'Well, I think that it is terribly hot down there, with flames all around, people getting tortured all the time until damnation, whatever that means. The devil dances on the bodies of evil men neither fully dead nor alive as their souls scream for release while he drinks the blood of the half-dead, and rivers of blood pour down the sides of Hell. Putrid brew is forced down people's throats, and the foul stench of rotting flesh is everywhere . . . ,' said Fletcher as he vaguely recollected some parts of Sunday mass.

'*Stop*! Stop! You are scaring me! Gosh, I think I am going to throw up!' exclaimed the Reaper with a shiver. Fletcher looked at him curiously.

'Mind explaining what you mean?' he asked impatiently, now totally confused by this reaction.

'Wait and see, my eager friend,' repeated the Reaper.

'Wisdom of the ages,' Fletcher sighed and sadly wondered just what was in store for him.

As time passed, the scenario changed. The clouds now became white, and there was a pleasant aroma all around. They kept travelling, moved by an unknown force in an uncertain direction. The sights grew more and more pleasant with hills of green grass and valleys of flowers. Butterflies of all colours flew around, and a rainbow appeared ahead. Fletcher was struck by the beauty of it all as he gazed open mouthed. After a few minutes, the beautiful and wonderful landscapes got better and better.

'Is this a guided tour of Heaven to show me what I will be missing before you take me to hell?' Fletcher inquired, bitterly.

The Reaper bent forward, doubled up, and laughed loudly while gripping his stomach. Making a supreme effort through his laughter he said, 'And . . . and . . . where do you think I picked you up from in the first place, my friend?' He collapsed, laughing and tumbling on the clouds under their feet. 'Smile! We have arrived!'

4

Swift Justice
(Based on an ancient Sanskrit tale)

THE CAT-BURGLAR SLOWLY crawled over the stone wall and jumped lightly into the grass below. It was about three hours before sunrise, and he knew that the entire village would be fast asleep at this time. He crept up to the two-storeyed house, taking shelter behind bushes where the house threw a large shadow, blocking the light from the full moon. A lone wolf howled somewhere in the mountains which set off some of the village dogs in matching their vocals with that of the wolf. The burglar spied the drain pipe running up on the side of the wall facing him. He grinned in satisfaction. He had made a recce every evening for the past week and had memorised every minute detail of this house. He had targeted this house specifically, as it belonged to a wealthy merchant who traded in spices with goods coming from Mesopotamia, Arabia, and Egypt. He had observed the merchant coming into the coastal village port of Kolaba, on the Arabian Sea coast, which lay at a distance of five days ride in a bullock cart, fully laden with his spices, several times in the past. It was a well-known fact in the village that the merchant was a wealthy man.

The burglar moved stealthily towards the drain pipe. Testing it with his hands, he started to climb. A few weeks back, he had overheard how a stone safe had been built by the village mason for the merchant and how it had required six persons to carry and install it. He was sure that the safe was located on the first floor, as he reasoned why six persons would have been needed to carry it. As he reached the top of the pipe, he leant over to grab hold of the window ledge from where he had planned to break in and enter. There was a sudden, loud crack and part of the clay pipe that he was holding on to crumpled while the remainder broke loose from its fittings running down the wall. The burglar frantically attempted to grab hold of the window ledge, but gravity did its work and the broken pipe, along with the burglar, collapsed to the ground, rendering him senseless.

The noise woke up the merchant and his family, and they quickly hastened to light candles and lanterns. His closest neighbours were too far away to have heard the sound. Arming himself with a stout stick, the merchant ran down the stone steps in his house and opened the door, while his elder son followed with a glowing oil lantern. When they reached around the house where the noise appeared to have come from, the merchant stumbled in the darkness over an obstruction and grunted in surprise as he fell to the ground. His son stopped dead in his tracks and held up the lantern, peering at his father in the soft glow of light. The short and portly merchant stood up, taking support from his son. Their eyes fell on the inert body of the burglar lying at their feet in the grass. They bent over the prostrate form and observed that the back of the victim's head was badly gashed, as blood flowed out from the wound. The younger son of the merchant had come out running by this time. Both sons lifted up the body while the merchant held up the lantern, and they took him inside the house. The merchant's wife shrieked in horror when she saw the blood stains on the hands and legs of her sons and their father. She calmed down a little when she saw that they were not hurt. They placed the unconscious form on a low divan, and the merchant urged his older son to run to the village for the doctor.

It was almost an hour before the only village doctor and his assistant reached the merchant's house. The victims wound had now been covered with cotton to arrest the bleeding.

'He looks to be in a bad condition,' said the doctor as he commenced his examination. 'Hmmm, severe head injury on the posterior area, fractured left ankle and left hand at the elbow, and probably more as well,' said the doctor as he completed his preliminary examination. 'He must be shifted to my hospital at once. Who is he, anyway?' queried the doctor as he peered at the unconscious form.

The merchant told the doctor how, upon hearing a crash outside the house, they had rushed out and found this stranger lying on the ground in this condition. The merchant's two sons and the doctor's assistant gently picked up the victim and placed him in the doctor's bullock-cart. The doctor insisted that the merchant's two sons accompany him to the hospital, until they had put the patient safely in bed. It was daybreak by the time the two boys returned home to their eagerly waiting parents. They had been unable to sleep after all the excitement. The merchant and his sons cleaned up the mess in their house and then proceeded outside to take a look at the scene of the strange occurrence of that night.

'Look, Father! The drain pipe from our terrace has come off,' said the older son as he looked up and down the wall. The crushed and broken section of the clay pipe lay close to the spot where they had found the stranger.

'My God! Then that fellow was nothing but a robber who was trying to get into the house!' exclaimed the merchant, visibly shaken. He stood rooted at his spot, trembling with horror, as he imagined what could have happened if the rascal had been successful. All his wealth lay in the stone safe that he had recently acquired and placed in his own room on the first floor. They might have even been murdered while they slept!

'Call the police,' ordered the merchant to his older son who immediately took to his heels. The village had three policemen, a head constable and two deputy constables. The policemen reached the merchant's house soon enough. The situation was explained to them by the merchant, while sipping hot tea that the merchant's wife had served.

The head constable was a tall and muscular fellow. What God had denied him in the cerebral area had been amply compensated in his massive physique. The merchant took them to the site of the incident behind the house.

'Hmmm, that there on the rock looks like blood,' said the head constable.

'That's right. That ruffian must have hit his head when he fell from the pipe,' said the merchant.

'I see no pipe on this wall, mister,' growled the head constable. The merchant looked at him in disbelief. 'But the remains of the pipe are right here where you see the blood!'

'How do I know that the man was not carrying a pipe with him and you assaulted the chap?'

The merchant could not believe what he had just heard.

'Are you accusing *me* of injuring the infernal robber? You must be crazy! I have never seen that man in my entire life. Look, I have told you everything just as it occurred. Don't you think that you are barking up the wrong tree?'

One of the deputy constables sniggered at this comment which earned him a sharp look from his senior.

'I am the head constable, and you will not speak that way to me! I will ask all the questions here and decide for myself what is true and what is not! Understood?'

The merchant calmed down immediately. He knew that this man was an illiterate brute who had obtained his position only because his father-in-law was the mayor of their hamlet, against whom he had voted in the last mayoral elections. In fact, the mayor knew this and was jealous of the merchant's prosperity.

'OK. OK. I am sorry. Please make your own assessment of the incident. I merely wanted to report an attempted robbery at my house. But please, do your own thing. I have been awake half the night, and I am tired. If you need me, I will be in my house,' said the merchant, fuming inwardly, as he turned to go back in his house.

'*Stop right there*! Make one move, and I will have you arrested for disobedience!'

The merchant froze in his tracks. He sighed and his shoulders drooped in weariness. The head constable eyed him suspiciously for a minute and then returned to his investigation. After four hours of incessant and completely irrelevant questions, the three policemen departed, heading for the hospital. The merchant went back into his house where his family awaited him to join them for lunch. After lunch, during which they discussed the curious episode of the previous night, the family decided to have a much-needed rest. They had barely fallen asleep when there were a series of sharp knocks on their door. The merchant groaned in his sleep-induced stupor and yawned. His wife got up swiftly muttering an oath and told her husband to go back to sleep while she checked who was making the fuss. The tired merchant nodded, lay back in bed, and immediately fell asleep. Hardly a few minutes had passed when he felt somebody or something poking his chest and shaking him. He moaned and sat up rubbing his tired eyes. He blinked in rapid succession as he saw the head constable with his two assistants standing next to his bed, while he saw his wife in the background voicing her protests. He immediately became alert. His sons had come running upon hearing the commotion.

'What's the matter now?' cried the merchant.

'Well, well, well! You have the nerve to sleep after committing such a vile deed. I must say you are a cool chap, assaulting a stranger who was just passing by! You really are in trouble this time,' said the head constable with a malignant smile on his face.

'Are you crazy? Where did you hear such nonsense?'

'Well, while you were sleeping, we of the police force have been busy. We have taken the statement from the poor stranger whom you claim to have attempted to rob you. He has formally registered a case against you from his hospital bed. Poor man! He could barely speak. But all the same, we recorded everything that he said on paper and then went with it to the judge to obtain an arrest warrant. By the power invested in me by the law of this hamlet, I arrest you on the basis of the stranger's evidence,' said the grim-faced head constable, solemnly.

The amazing turn of events shocked the merchant out of his wits. A loud wail echoed from the other side of the room where the merchant's wife sat while her sons looked on numb and distressed at what they had just heard. The policemen tied the still dazed merchant's hands with a thick rope and led him out of the house and then to the courthouse on foot. It was a very uncommon sight in the hamlet. They had never experienced seeing anyone being arrested and humiliated. As the news spread, it brought people running onto the streets to see the curious sight for themselves. Upon reaching the courthouse, the judge immediately confirmed the arrest and ordered that the merchant should be incarcerated in the tiny cell at the police station and scheduled the trial for the morning of the following day.

The next day, the dishevelled prisoner was brought into the courthouse in the morning which was already packed by the entire population of the hamlet. The hubbub of conversation was deafening until the judge arrived and banged his wooden gavel on his desk, calling for order. In those ancient times, there were no juries or prosecutors or defence lawyers. There was just a Council of Seven wise old men who now sat on a bench, one step below the judge's chair. It was generally believed and accepted that all old and hoary or bald men were the wisest. The bald judge was the oldest of the lot and was elected by the Council of The Seven Wise Men.

'Bring the prisoner and have him stand in front of us,' ordered the judge to the head constable. This was immediately complied with. The judge cleared his throat and looked with displeasure at the huge gathering.

'You, merchant, have been charged with causing bodily harm to an innocent stranger last night. The facts will be presented to the court by the head constable after which the doctor will be called in to give evidence. But, before we proceed, do you have anything to say?'

'Your Honour! I have done nothing wrong! I and my family were asleep on that fateful night when we heard a loud noise. We got up to investigate and found the stranger lying on the ground behind my house. We immediately treated the stranger's wounds and called the doctor who took him away to his hospital for treatment. In the morning, we checked around the house for clues and found the drain pipe, which leads from my terrace, broken and shattered into pieces, lying exactly where the stranger was found. I immediately concluded that the stranger had attempted to climb the drain pipe, which runs along the back wall of my house, with the intention of robbing me! The pipe must have broken during his misadventure, and he must have fallen, which caused his injuries. Your Honour, I am a respectable merchant and have always followed the law. I am not to blame in this case as I had nothing to do with the injuries to the stranger!' said the merchant emotionally, with tears in his eyes. His family, sitting in the front rows, gave him a sad but encouraging smile.

'I understand your position, merchant. Nevertheless, it is the stranger who has claimed damages against you and also accuses you of causing him bodily harm, in writing. The case will proceed on this basis,' said the judge and banged his gavel on the desk. The seven wise old men nodded their heads in agreement, as they sat with their eyes half-closed. There were murmurs all around the courtroom, which were immediately silenced by another rap of the gavel.

'Head constable, kindly share the findings of your investigation with this court.'

The head constable puffed up his chest in a pompous show of his importance and stood before the court.

'Your Holiness, I and my two deputies have worked very hard since yesterday morning without food or sleep so as to carry out a thorough investigation.'

He paused and looked around the courtroom as if he expected applause from the onlookers. Annoyed, that there was no response, he continued, 'I was summoned to the merchant's house yesterday morning by one of his sons, who claimed that there had been an attempted robbery at their house. He said nothing about the injured man until I was at the site and found blood on a stone in the backyard. The merchant seemed most concerned about his broken drain pipe rather than the health and well-being of the stranger. This immediately made me suspicious. After cross-questioning the merchant, he stated that he merely wanted to report an attempted robbery! I then went to the hospital where the doctor explained the injuries suffered by the stranger. Just then, the stranger regained consciousness and immediately gave his statement in which he claimed that he wished to make a case against the merchant. His statement with his signature has already been submitted before you, Your Holiness. We then came to you for a warrant for arresting the merchant and then arrested him,' said the head constable. The seven sagacious old men continued nodding their heads in unison.

'Thank you and your men, head constable, for a fine job. I will now read out the stranger's evidence as it is of utmost importance,' said the judge. He again cleared his throat before speaking.

'I, a stranger to your beautiful hamlet, was just passing through last night, when I observed a magnificent house located on the outskirts of your village. As I am interested in architecture, I wanted to have a closer look to see this amazing construction. However, as I was climbing up a drain pipe to take a closer look at the intricate designs on the back wall near the first floor, the pipe broke and I fell down from a height, due to which I have suffered several grievous injuries. I hold the merchant solely responsible for my injuries and claim ten kilos of gold as compensation.'

The crowd, hearing the claim, got excited and started a loud discussion, which earned them a series of gavel strikes by the judge. The merchant gasped at the fantastic story. He looked across at the seven old men and saw them nodding again, with their eyes half-closed.

'Your Honour! That is just pure nonsense!' shouted the irate merchant.

'Silence!' roared the judge. 'You shall not speak until permitted to, understand?'

The merchant became uneasy but decided to keep quiet, having seen his wife looking at him while putting one finger across her lips, as if to tell her husband to keep quiet.

'Call the doctor, as the final witness,' ordered the judge. Once the doctor took the stand, he was asked for his observations. The doctor rambled on for long about the injuries and finally stated that the injuries were very severe. The judge then turned to the wise old men.

'What does the respected Council of Seven have to say about what they have heard?' asked the judge, looking at the nodding sages. A whispered conference was quickly held between the seven, and one of them, with a hunched back and a long, white beard which almost touched the ground, got up to speak.

'We, of the Council of Seven, find the merchant guilty of having installed poor quality of drain pipes which was the main cause leading to the injuries of the young stranger,' he said in a quavering, high-pitched voice.

The crowd roared with jubilation. 'What a quick verdict! How sagacious the Council of Seven,' thought the crowd, while the merchant's family wept in frustration.

'Order, order! Are there any grounds on which we may reconsider the verdict?' asked the judge to the Council of Seven. They shook their sagacious heads, again simultaneously, eyes firmly closed. The judge banged his gavel on the desk and proceeded with the verdict.

'On the basis of evidence produced and the advice of the Council of Seven, I direct the merchant to pay the stranger ten kilograms of pure gold by tomorrow morning in this court, in front of myself and the Council of Seven, as witnesses. Until then, the prisoner shall remain in the custody of the police,' he said and banged the gavel loudly, one last time, which startled and woke up the seven old men.

'Your Honour! Ten kilos of gold! I will barely have half of that amount and that too if I sell my house and all my possessions. What am I to do?' cried the poor merchant, pulling at his sparse hair. His family was shocked and cried openly. The head constable took charge of his prisoner and led him back to the cell, while the crowd booed and threw tomatoes and eggs at the merchant, just as the sun was setting.

It was early in the morning next day, just when the sun was about to rise that there was a loud hammering on the door of the police station. At night, only one deputy constable manned the police station and that too because there was a prisoner in the cell now. He got up slowly and went to open the door. The doctor stood in front of the deputy, out of breath as if he had come running from his hospital. He gasped for breath while the wide-eyed deputy looked on in confusion.

'Cal . . . huuuuuh . . . call . . . hoooofff . . . your boss . . . patient . . . died . . . ooooofff . . . few minutes ago,' the doctor managed to say, completely exhausted from his sprint. The deputy's eyes widened in disbelief. He opened his mouth to say something, but nothing came out. Controlling his emotions, he took a deep breath, nodded, and said, 'Stay right here, doctor, while I fetch the chief.'

He ran out as if his clothes were on fire. Within a few minutes, the head constable appeared, red-eyed, dishevelled, and still under the influence of his last night's indulgence.

'Doctor! Is it true? My God! My God! My first murder case! This is just fantastic! OK, doctor, you can now go back to your hospital and take care of the dead stranger. Hurry! Make sure that he is safe, OK? We will need you at the court again today, so be prepared,' said the head constable. The doctor muttered an oath under his breath and walked back slowly towards his hospital, shaking his head.

It took the policemen a long time to gather up all the seven wise men and the judge since they had been up most of the night, revelling in the aftermath of a successful verdict of one of the rare and few cases they had experienced in the last few years. Five of the seven were found just before noon, still in a stupor, with their arms and legs intertwined with those of their consorts of the night, at a place infamous for the practice of the oldest profession in the world, which was located just outside the village.

The judge and the two remaining old men were finally found at noon at the mayor's house, in a similar state of drunkenness.

It was late in the afternoon by the time the red-eyed Council of Seven and the judge assembled in the courthouse. Exactly as before, the courtroom was packed almost to the ceiling with the villagers.

'Order, order. Bring the prisoner in front of the council,' directed the judge to the head constable who still had a bad case of hiccups. The merchant was brought before the court, and he stood wearily with his head bowed and shoulders slumped. No one had an inkling of the astonishing news of that morning.

'Merchant! There has been a grave turn of events. The stranger has died this morning due to his injuries. Because of this, it is now a murder case. You are hereby charged with the offence of manslaughter. How do you plead?' thundered the judge. The merchant had given a start of surprise when he heard of the stranger's death. He almost fainted when he heard the judge telling him that he was now labelled a murderer. The crowd burst out into an angry roar. Taking his gavel, the judge hammered away on his desk consistently to silence the crowd. It was almost half an hour before the crowd quietened down and the court came to order. The hushed crowd waited for the prisoner to speak.

'Merchant! What do you have to say?' repeated the judge.

In a choked voice, the merchant said, 'Not guilty, my lord, not guilty.'

His family burst into tears and wailed loudly which caused a sharp comment from the judge to behave themselves, or they would be thrown out.

'How does the Council of Seven see the new development in this case?' asked the judge.

The seven old men put their hung-over heads together and whispered amongst themselves for a few minutes. A bald-headed old man with a short white beard stood up, supporting himself on the shoulder of an even older man, sitting by his side.

'We, the Council of Seven, find that the prisoner is responsible for the death of the stranger. We also urge the judge to take the mayor into confidence and request his view, since the punishment for murder is death by hanging and we do not want to be solely responsible for giving this verdict,' said the old man while holding his throbbing head with the other hand.

The crowd again burst into a roar, this time of solid approval. Many threw their caps into the air in jubilation. The merchant's wife screamed and fainted while her sons held up her inert body, too shocked to react. The poor quivering merchant fell down in a faint. The extraordinarily proportioned mayor stood up. He was not a man to go against the crowd or the council who had a hand in making him what he was. In any case, he hated the merchant.

He gazed all around the courtroom and said, 'I agree, as the Honourable Mayor of this hamlet, that the prisoner should be hung by his neck, until his death.'

He had no guts to deny the judge or the Council of Seven their verdict. Each of them was interdependent and had to move as a cohesive force. Any lapse would mean that one of them would be out of the safe and secure cocoon of superiority and power. The head constable motioned his two deputies to take the prisoner away.

As the semi-conscious form of the merchant was being dragged away, the crowd had now resorted to throwing stones and bricks at the prisoner, which rarely struck the prisoner, but mostly his gaolers. The bleeding duo with their dazed charge finally reached the execution platform as the crowds shouted slogans against the merchant vociferously. A masked hangman stood by, with apprehension clearly visible in spite of his masked face. This was not only the first hanging that he would be personally administering, but also the first that he would ever see! He was extremely nervous but held high hopes of pleasing the crowd that had now gathered around. After all, he told himself, his father had been an unsuccessful doctor by trade, so such a task would not be too difficult for him. The presence of the head constable, who had followed the prisoner, had an electrifying effect on the hangman. The entire procession was followed by the Council of Seven, accompanied by the judge and the mayor, who looked at each other gravely. The sun was now close to setting, as the prisoner was pushed onto the wooden scaffolding by the eager hands of the two deputies, while the noose swung about lazily in the wind. He reluctantly climbed up on a tall wooden stool as the hangman held him by one arm. The crowd became excited and hysterical and started shouting slogans against the merchant, over and over. The merchant's wife, supported by her sons, stood in a corner near the scaffold, weeping profusely as she looked up at her poor husband, dejectedly. They had lost. The head constable looked at the judge who nodded back at him. The head constable then spoke sharply to the hangman to proceed.

The hangman, holding the noose, quickly reached forward to put it around the merchant's neck while the crowd cheered him on. As he pulled on the noose, he suddenly stopped short, shocked out of his wits. The noose would not go any further! The merchant appeared to be too short for the length of the rope which had to reach his neck! The crowd fell silent when they saw this. The merchant and his family were past caring and continued to weep hysterically. The alarmed hangman looked around for support and advice, concerned with how he was to perform his duties when he saw that the Council of Seven, the judge, and the mayor were also looking at him, completely bewildered!

'What is the matter, hangman? Why have you stopped?' asked the irate judge.

'You have nothing to be afraid of, my man, just do what you have been asked to do!' followed the Mayor.

'S . . . sss . . . ir, the noose, . . . is . . . t . . . ttt . . . too sh . . . s . . . sshort for the p . . . p . . . pprisoner!' stammered the mortified hangman.

The crowd growled furiously, scenting that they were being stood up from witnessing a conclusive argument. Desperately, the mayor looked at the judge and then at the Council of Seven, for some guidance. They were dumb with amazement. Nobody had foreseen this eventuality and none of them were sure how to proceed. He finally motioned the judge to take over before things got out of hand.

The judge caught the mayor's signal, stood up immediately, and shouted at the crowd, 'People of the hamlet, we need to ensure that all elements of our laws have been applied before the final justice is served. Please give us a few minutes to confer.'

The crowd was stunned and started a debate within. The merchant, standing swaying on the stool with his eyes closed, was praying to all the Gods, asking for a smooth transition from the earth to wherever they desired, while he was flanked by the two assistant constables and the hangman stood off to one side scratching his head, wondering how things had gone wrong with the hanging. The Council of Seven, the mayor, the judge, and the head constable stood on the other side of the platform and put their heads together and a whispered discussion started.

'What the hell! How do we continue with the hanging? The rope is too short, isn't it? Can something be done or should we cancel it?' asked the mayor, overtly alarmed that crowd behind him was getting restless.

The judge made an angry noise and burst out, 'No way! This is my first verdict for murder, and I intend to make sure that the hanging takes place, come what may. It will ruin all our reputations if we do not carry out the hanging!

Does anyone know how this has happened?' They all fell silent, inwardly thinking how the situation could still be saved.

One of the senior-most from the Council of Seven spoke up, 'The last time that we have had a hanging in this village was more than fifty years ago. I was a young man of thirty then. The man who was hanged was six feet three inches tall, which is why we are stuck in this position.'

The Judge became curious and asked, 'Who was he?'

'Oh, nobody important. Just the local rope-maker. If I recollect, he was hanged because his ropes were found too short when we tried to use them to save people during the floods,' said the old man, nonchalantly.

Hearing this, the dim-witted head constable's eyes widened as he recollected something. The head constable felt that he must put in two bits of his wisdom or else he would look foolish in front of them. 'This is just terrible. The bloody merchant is at least a foot shorter than the noose. What terrible luck! What a pity that it's our village barber who is six feet three inches tall, instead of the merchant! I am sure of this! He always complains about how his back aches when he has to bend over forward while cutting people's hair,' said the head constable, offhandedly.

This astounding piece of information surprised them all, and they looked at him in amazement. The mayor looked at his son-in-law thoughtfully. He had always imagined him to be a dim-witted oaf, but today, the boy had surpassed them all! Maybe, just maybe, his son-in-law could succeed him as mayor when he retired, mused the mayor.

'Brilliant! Just brilliant, my boy!' exclaimed the mayor with wonder and respect in his eyes. The judge and the Council of Seven broke out of their momentary stun and patted the head constable on his back for the wonderful idea. The head constable felt confused at this adulation. All he had stated was a fact and now he was being looked at with praise in their eyes. However, he managed to keep a straight face and decided to bask in his moment of glory. The judge looked at the mayor and smiled. The mayor smiled back and nodded. They both looked at the Council of Seven who looked relieved and smiled back, nodding their approval. The mayor whispered a few words into his son-in-law's ear, who immediately nodded, threw a hap-hazard salute, and rushed off to do the mayor's bidding. The judge took the lead and climbed up the stage where the hanging was to take place.

Holding up his hands for silence, he said, 'Justice demands that the execution take place as scheduled. As the rightful upholders of the law, we will ensure that justice is served. I ask you all to bear with me for a few minutes.'

The crowd appeared mollified and gave their approval vociferously. The sobbing family of the poor merchant wailed in unison.

Meanwhile, the head constable had been busy and out of sight. The sun was now touching the horizon. Within a few minutes, the murmuring crowd fell silent as they heard a new sound of wailing behind them. They turned around to find the village barber being dragged at the end of a rope by the head constable. It was an uneven match since the head constable was well ahead in the weight category but fell short by two inches in height. The procession drew oaths of derision and merriment amongst those gathered as the barber was dragged up to the scaffold. With a rude push, the merchant was thrust aside, and he fell off the platform in a cloud of dust close to where his family stood, numb with disbelief.

'Hear me now and hear me well,' shouted the judge, who had now ascended the scaffold with the mayor in tow. 'As promised, we shall have a hanging right here and right now. Justice shall be served in accordance with the tenets of our belief and as per the wishes of the crowd,' roared the judge, to yells of 'bravo, long live justice'.

The mayor quickly motioned to the head constable to fix the noose around the barber's neck. This was accomplished with a little difficulty, since the barber's height was perfect for the noose, although he continued to protest loudly. As soon as the noose was fitted around the barber's neck, the judge gave a signal to the hangman, who immediately kicked away the stool on which the barber stood.

All of them watched with rapt fascination in the dimming light, to the spasmodic reaction of the barber's involuntary bodily movements as the noose snapped his spinal cord. After a few minutes, the barber's body hung inert, dangling freely at the end of the rope. Pin-drop silence prevailed across those gathered, their eyes fixated on the gory sight. The doctor stepped up to the scaffold, checked the pulse of the hanging body, and pronounced him dead. The entire crowd yelled in celebration, beating drums and dancing. Fire-crackers were lit, and their noise added to the humongous crescendo of the celebrating crowds. The merchant and his family had already departed the scene, eager to get out of the crazy village with their belongings. The judge, mayor, head constable and the Council of Seven looked on proudly at the way they had ensured that justice was served, as well as the continuity of their positions, while the body of the poor barber swung eerily in the gust of the evening wind.

5

Saddam's Legacy

THE GROUP OF soldiers quietly entered the ancient courtyard which was strewn with broken-down mud walls and debris of what had once been a house, their eyes darting left and right for the slightest signs of danger and guns ready for immediate use. Captain Jacobs was the man in charge of this band of highly trained fighters who were all ex-US Special Forces and had been hand-picked by the chief of one of the largest oil companies in the world. Extermination without record was their specialty. Each man was listed as MIA in Iraq about two years ago. The job they were now involved in was to search for an entrance to an underground tunnel. It was Saddam who had in fact opened a can of worms when he was being interrogated after his capture in December 2003. In a fit of bravado and under the effect of Sodium Pentothal, he had again claimed to have in his possession the 'Mother of all weapons'. This had triggered an enormous amount of speculation worldwide and consternation in the uppermost echelons of NATO. The term 'Mother of all Weapons' had led to the assumption that he had been ranting about a nuclear bomb. It had been evident from the regular CIA field reports from Iraq that Saddam's scientists had been working as discreetly as possible to develop a nuclear weapon. However, the progress had been reported as comically slow, to the extent that a senator had joked during a presidential briefing that there was a distinct possibility that Iraq would have the bomb ready at least by end of human civilisation, if not later. The joke had blown up badly in his face the next morning when he read his morning brief and heard of Saddam's disclosure of the term 'Mother of all Weapons' and much to his dismay become the butt of everyone's ridicule. The real answer was never found, and Saddam was executed anyway.

It was a retired professor of archaeology who had received a curious email from one of his ex-students. Alan Rice, the ex-student, had been hired by the Smithsonian Institute to go to Iraq in April 2004, with a dozen other archaeologists to take an inventory of whatever remained in the fabulous Baghdad Museum after Saddam's fall. Almost 14,000 artefacts had been stolen within a thirty-six-hour period, after the war had broken out. Rice, who worked at George Washington University in Washington DC as an associate research analyst, had literally tumbled into a well-hidden, crudely sealed-off tunnel under the catacombs of the Baghdad Museum late one evening, having lost his way in the labyrinthine underground passageways. He had found a relatively new, locked steel box which was completely out of place in this part of the ancient Museum. He had broken the lock which bore Saddam's personal seal and had found the box filled with eighteen scrolls made out of parchment, the likes of which he had never seen before.

The scrolls had curious markings in what appeared to him to be written in the Sumerian cuneiform script. Knowing that Professor Berkley was one of the few persons who was an expert in transliteration of ancient cuneiform scripts, he had hidden the parchments in his bags and smuggled them back into the US after completing the task he had come for in Iraq in August 2004. At the airport, the Customs and Border Protection personnel were not interested in what looked like old papers. They had been told to be on alert for a biological or chemical attack from Saddam's few remaining admirers.

Alan Rice had immediately gone to Cleveland where his retired professor lived. He had called ahead to warn the professor that he was on his way to meet him. The professor, now in his mid-fifties, was happy and surprised to be visited by one of his favourite students.

'Good evening, Alan-my-boy,' said Professor Berkley warmly, 'what a pleasant surprise to see you after all these years! How long has it been, two years?' Alan nodded.

'Thank you, professor,' said Alan Rice, inwardly amused at being called a boy at his age of thirty-six. 'How have you been? Win anything on roulette?' asked Alan, knowing the old man's gambling habits.

'Well, you win some and you lose some. Care for a drink?' he asked Alan who said he wouldn't mind a neat Scotch. The professor got a bottle of finest Glenmorangie and two glasses from a huge bar. 'So, are you married now or still single?' he asked as he uncorked the bottle.

'Still, very much a bachelor. No girl wants to move in with a guy who is passionate about old mummies,' said Alan with a wide grin. The professor laughed at this old joke.

'Long time since I heard that one, Alan,' he said while pouring out the golden liquid into the two glasses. He handed over one to Alan.

'Cheers, professor,' said Alan, which was acknowledged by Dr Berkley. They both took a big sip of the fine brew, savouring its delightful aftermath.

'Don't tell me that you came all the way here for my Scotch or that you are planning to stay with me, seeing those bags you have got with you,' said the professor. Alan merely opened one of his bags which was lying near his feet and took out the eighteen scrolls, keeping them rolled up on the sofa beside him. The professor eyed these curiously from behind his thick glasses.

The professor's impatience gave way, and he got up to study what was laid out on the sofa. 'So, what do we have here? Is that parchment?' he said as he came closer and peered at the rolls of parchment.

'Let's take this to your study,' said Alan and followed the professor as he led him to his study which was filled with volumes of books all around the mahogany panelled bookcase, leaving one place for a curtained window and one place for the door through which they had entered. The professor cleared his desk above which was a lampshade made of clay with exotic oriental carvings. Alan laid out the sheaf of scrolls on the table and rolling them open, placed four paperweights on each corner. Dr Berkley went around the table and joined him.

'These are scrolls that I literally stumbled upon, while I was in Iraq taking an inventory of artefacts in the ancient Museum of Baghdad. I know the script is Sumerian but cannot make much out of it, so I thought you would be the best person to ask,' explained Alan quietly.

'You mean to say that you *stole* these from the museum?' cried the professor in amazement. 'I thought very highly of you, Alan!' said the professor mockingly. Over the years, the professor had discreetly amassed several precious artefacts from around the world. He maintained a high-class lifestyle by selling one or two pieces once in a while, whenever he was short of cash through a dealer of stolen artwork who took a 50 per cent cut from the proceeds. His maximum earning through any sale was in the upper six figures, so this did not require him to sell stuff frequently. Since his retirement five years ago, he had needed to sell only four artefacts which had kept him under the radar of law enforcement agencies. His modest house and car did not attract much attention. He only spent on the world's finest scotch and cigars, gambling in Macau and the regular visits to certain places of ill-repute in diverse places from Thailand to Brazil. Alan was the one and only ex-student who knew the professor's weaknesses and had actually been part of a few of the earlier scams.

Alan grinned back at the professor and said, 'Thought if this was really worthwhile, I could maybe retire from work and settle down.'

The professor chuckled and leaned over the scrolls, peering through his spectacles. Dr Berkley exclaimed as he saw the writing on the scrolls. He suddenly appeared to have shed his retirement-induced lethargic movements and started moving around the room rapidly. He ran to a bookshelf and picked out three volumes, throwing them at an amazed Alan to catch, and then hurrying to a corner of the room, he opened a drawer from which he took out a powerful magnifying lens. For the next nine hours, Dr Berkley and Alan studied each and every single parchment carefully while Dr Berkley scribbled a few notes on a large notepad, occasionally referring to one of the volumes. There was whispered discussion between the two occasionally followed by long periods of silence during which time the pendulum of the clock sounded like a crescendo of slow drumbeats. The whiskey and dinner were long forgotten affairs, and Alan was mesmerised by the professor's activity and focus on the study of the parchments.

The professor looked blankly at Alan as if he was seeing him for the first time in the room. 'Alan, I need at least a week to ensure that I can interpret all these scrolls correctly before I have something concrete. All I can say at this stage is that I suspect this could be the most wonderful find ever. Look, it is early morning now. I feel completely exhausted, and I am sure that you do as well. When do you have to return to work?' he asked.

'I can take a break for a week or two. I was away on the field trip to Iraq for almost four months, so there is a long leave due to me,' said Alan.

'No. You get back to work and just get involved in your normal routine. Do not reveal anything of this to anyone.' Dr Berkley paused, thinking hard, 'On second thoughts, take two weeks leave. Tell them you are sick or something. Stay here with me. The lesser you expose yourself, the better we will be able to keep this from getting out.'

Alan called the head of his department and asked him for a week of medical leave which was granted unenthusiastically. He then went out and purchased some clothes and toiletries sufficient to last him for a month. The two men continued to work incessantly on the parchments, from dusk to dawn and then after a few hours of sleep, continue at noon until early evening. They would then have a quick meal washed down with scotch and water and then at dusk resume their study. After six days, Alan called the University and reported that he was still sick. He promised his boss that he would come back to work as soon as he was better.

The two men continued working hectically for the next two weeks. In the early morning of the thirteenth day, an exhausted professor at last sighed tiredly and collapsed into a huge armchair in the corner.

'Pour me a tumbler-full of that single malt, Alan, and sit down,' said the red-eyed professor in a quivering voice. 'Do you know what this is, my boy?' he asked as he took the tumbler of scotch from Alan with a shaky hand. 'This is the zenith of human achievements. The final frontier.

The wisdom of the ancients. The mother of all inventions. There can be no more than this. And to think that this was available to us all the time, all throughout time,' said a completely dazed and forlorn-looking Dr Berkley.

Both had lost a significant amount of weight due to their poor eating habits. Alan looked at the professor, waiting impatiently for an explanation. When there was none coming, he looked down into his glass and took a large sip for inspiration. He had understood the basic ideology of the parchments but nothing that actually made sense.

When he saw that the professor was frozen into his chair and was muttering to himself, he asked wearily, 'So what do the parchments say, professor? I could make out that the parchments depict directions for something, and there are references to magnetism, solar rays, and specific metals like gold. The drawings appear to be some sort of a design for constructing something. Am I right, professor?'

'Close enough but not sufficient,' said Dr Berkley. He took off his glasses and passed a gnarled old hand over his weary eyes. He had deliberately kept his handwritten notes away from Alan's reach.

'Mind letting me in on it?' asked Alan impatiently. The professor looked across at Alan slyly and said, 'I propose a fifty-fifty partnership first.'

'That's all right with me. What do you think it is worth?' replied Alan without any hesitation. The professor appeared pleased and said, 'All right, listen up. This thing is priceless. Whoever owns the secret is really the ruler of the world. Damn! This is indeed the best find of the millennium! Still, we are not looking for being world rulers, so I reckon we can get a couple of million dollars at the least.'

Alan sucked in a deep breath and gave a sharp exclamation. A couple of million dollars!

'I know that you are dying to know what the text and diagrams mean. Trust me, it will be safer if only one of us knows what it is. In any case that will be my only insurance against you trying to kill me once you know what this is,' said the professor slyly, with a smile.

Alan nodded and laughed at the sinister joke. He had actually started thinking on those lines anyway. Still, the old man was known to keep his word and had always done so with Alan in the past. The sale of a rare set of coins dating back to the time of Alexander the Great which Alan had discreetly picked up from a dig-site in north-western Pakistan five years ago and sold through the professor had given him a share of 25,000 dollars. But this was different.

'Here's what we do. You will go back to work immediately, and I will come to Washington the day after tomorrow. We will keep in touch by cell phone. You have my number. Never mention the scrolls at any time. We don't know who might listen in. I will contact my cousin who works in Washington at the White House. He owes me a favour and takes me and my professional work seriously. I will ask him to arrange a meeting with the president, if possible. I know he is in town,' said Dr Berkley. 'You will join me on 27, which is a Friday, at the Hillside Motel which is just an hour's drive outside town, to the west'.

'What? Why the government? They will never listen to us or pay us! Bloody hell! I never thought you of all people would fall for that!'

'Look son. It's not only about the money. This thing is so big that whether we like it or not, we will get rewarded with enough to last us a lifetime because of the nature of what we are about to reveal. This will be legitimate money. We will never have to dip anywhere again as long as we live. Look at the additional perks. We will be legally famous, help the entire world, and still be rich. What else would anyone ever want?' asked Dr Berkley, seriously. Alan calmed down but had doubt written all over his face.

'I am still not sure. Also, what if they ask us where I got these scrolls in the first place? I think this is a bad idea,' said Alan, nervously.

The professor stood up and walked over to Alan. He took Alan's shoulders in his hands, 'Trust me, Alan. I have nothing but our best interests at heart. I know what will happen if we try to take any other course. So just once, trust me, OK?'

Alan still looked upset but finally gave in. 'All right, professor. I will go along with what you say. I will leave this evening for Washington. But how do we explain these parchments, where I got them?' asked Alan.

'Don't worry about that. I will think of something,' said the professor fiercely. 'Now remember. We cannot make it obvious to anyone that we have hit the mother lode.'

'Take it easy, professor. I understand,' said Alan in a placating tone. He wondered what story the professor was going to cook up to explain how the parchments had landed up in his hands. He yawned loudly while scratching the sixteen-day stubble on his chin. 'I think I will crash out for a few hours before I leave, if that's OK with you.'

'Of course, my boy. I think I will just sit here and plan the next steps.'

Alan went into the hall and stretched out on the sofa and soon fell fast asleep. The professor lit up a cigar and settled down with a glass of scotch, looking blankly at the wall in front of him. He had to make up a convincing story. At last, he would be able to live respectably and without guilt. Except Alan. 'He would have to be sacrificed,' thought the professor without remorse. He was not ready to share the glory with anyone.

That evening, before Alan left for Washington, the professor discussed his plan with Alan. The next morning, he made three calls, two to Washington and one to New York. The first one was to his cousin in the White House to arrange a meeting with the president, and the second was to book a cabin at the Hillside Inn. The last call was to a certain American 'gentleman' whom he had met a few years back in Macau during one of his gambling trips. The professor had bailed the 'gentleman' out of a huge loss while gambling at the high stakes tables and they had become friends. Over drinks, the 'gentleman' had revealed that his speciality was extermination for a price, to be paid after a job was done.

When his calls were completed, he sat down in his favourite armchair and thought; the first step had been taken. It was only a matter of a few hours at the most before things would start to move at a breathless pace. He smiled to himself and started translating the entire contents of the scrolls into plain English. By midnight, he finished the job and retired to bed. Waking up early next morning, he got ready and packed a suitcase. He took a taxi to the airport and then, the first available flight to Washington. At Dulles airport, he hailed a cab and reached the Hillside Inn Motel, about two hours later. Having settled down in his small cottage which was located at the end of a row of other cottages, he made a call to his cousin in Washington to confirm the time of the meeting. Then he called Alan, gave him directions to his motel, and asked him to come down the next morning in his best suit.

Alan reached the motel around 11 a.m. the following day and went straight to the professor's cabin.

'Why the heck did you pick up a room in a dump like this! I thought we were going to be rich!' asked Alan, extremely annoyed. He had taken a couple of wrong turns while searching for this out-of-nowhere place.

'Sit down, Alan,' said a well-attired Dr Berkley, in a tweed suit befitting his profession, from a chair next to a writing table. He motioned him to take the other chair. Alan sat down.

'C'mon, professor, I have been unable to sleep these last two nights. Tell me what's been happening.'

'All right then. This is a totally isolated place and is discreetly located, that's why I selected it. Here's the deal. I called my cousin at the White House. He has arranged for us to be picked up at noon today for a meeting with the president, scheduled for 4 p.m. There will be two men from the Secret Service here in a SUV. We have only been scheduled for a five-minute meeting, but I have a feeling that the president will be cancelling all his appointments today once he hears us out,' said the professor, smiling.

'Where are the scrolls, professor?' asked Alan.

'Safely in my briefcase. I have prepared a translation as well, complete with easy to understand diagrams,' said the professor.

The two made small talk as they waited for the appointed hour. Five minutes before noon, they heard two vehicles pulling up the steep incline leading to the motel. Peering out from his window, Dr Berkley saw two huge black SUVs screeching to a halt in front of their cabin. Two men got down and quickly ran up the steps leading to the front door and barged their way into his room, after knocking on the door.

'Dr Berkley? I am Special Agent Dickson, and this is Special Agent Davis. We have instructions to escort you and Mr Rice to the White House,' said a tall, dark man who had called himself Dickson. The professor looked at him and nodded.

'If you gents will allow me to pick up a few things, we should be off in a minute,' said the professor. Dr Berkley picked up his briefcase and headed for the door. He was stopped by Dickson while Davis remained at a distance, alert and watchful. Dickson expertly frisked Alan and the professor and finally the briefcase within two minutes.

'Please follow me, gentlemen,' said Dickson after he was satisfied that the duo were not carrying any weapons and made his way towards the first SUV. Davis followed behind them as Dickson opened the rear door for the duo to enter. As soon as they were inside, he slammed the door shut and got into the front seat. Davis got into the second vehicle, and both cars drove off at a high speed. The driver of the first car was dressed in a similar fashion as Dickson. The two cars sped along at a high speed and reached the freeway. The professor immediately saw that they had turned away from the city and felt confused.

'Hey! We are going the wrong way,' exclaimed the surprised professor. There was no reply from the two Secret Service agents except that Dickson had turned in his seat and was pointing a gun at him.

'What the hell is going on,' the professor snarled, turning to Alan and saw the look in Alan's eyes. There was no emotion in them. A cold smile on his face betrayed the fact that Alan had a different agenda. These were no Secret Service agents!

'Why, Alan? Why?' cried Dr Berkley in an agonised, emotion-choked voice. 'Do you even know what you had discovered?'

'Yes, professor. I saw what you had written down on your notepad when you were asleep. You know, I want much more than just recognition. And you? You thought that I would be the fall guy? How were you going to explain, how I got those scrolls? You were going to get me arrested, weren't you? You think I am stupid?! Here, give me that bag!' snarled Alan, viciously, and snatched the briefcase out of Dr Berkley's hands. The professor gave up the bag without a fight, trembling with fright. 'I should have gotten Alan out of the way earlier,' thought the professor, bitterly.

'Is it there?' asked Dickson. Alan tore open the briefcase and took out the translation. Flicking through the pages, Alan nodded. After a few miles, the two cars turned off the freeway and entered a thickly wooded area. Two miles later, the convoy stopped near a flowing creek covered with foliage on a hill slope. The so-called Secret Service agents forced the professor out at gunpoint.

'Goodbye, asshole. I am not sorry it has to end this way for you. But rather you than me,' said Alan without any remorse from his back seat in the SUV. The professor turned around and looked forlornly at Alan with tears in his eyes. No words came from his open mouth. The fake agents quietly guided him towards the trees. After ten minutes, two muffled shots were heard. An hour later, the three agents came back brushing the dirt off their clothes.

'All done?' asked Alan.

'Yeah. You sure that the documents are all in order?' inquired Davis.

'Yes. This is the entire translation. Let's hurry now,' said Alan impatiently. He was trembling with eager anticipation of spending all that money that he had got, for double-crossing the professor. He had read enough of what the professor had written on his notepad when the professor was asleep and he knew who would pay him money immediately.

As soon as they got back into their SUVs, they raced off towards the city. Dickson made the call to the other side of Washington and gave an ETA of two hours.

Two hours and thirty minutes later, the chief, as he was known, sat back in his comfortable office chair on the fifty-second floor of the company building with Professor Berkley's briefcase by his side, the original manuscript of eighteen pages on his desk and the translation in his hands. He called his secretary and told her that he was not to be disturbed for the remaining part of the day. With a glass of water by his side, he commenced reading. After three hours, he whistled softly as he put down the translation, lost in wonder. He got up and walked towards the glass wall which overlooked the Potomac. So this was what he had been searching for all these years! His troops of ex-forces had searched everywhere in Iraq but had returned empty-handed. The secret of Saddam's 'Mother of all Weapons' was finally in his hands. And what a weapon it had turned out to be! He was glad that Alan Rice had called his office and had negotiated a price for this amazing secret, which he had been searching for. Alan had met Captain Jacobs in Iraq, who was discreetly trying to find out if the archaeological teams had found anything strange. Alan had been instrumental in giving details of the professor's movements, so the chief had got the phone in the motel room tapped. The call from the professor to his cousin had been taken by one of his henchmen, sitting on top of a telephone pole, 100 metres away from the cottage. 'Funny,' he thought, 'how the professor had not noticed the change in the voice at the other end of the telephone.' He looked at his watch. He had paid a million dollars in cash to Alan last evening. He smiled. It was the cheapest investment that he had ever made.

The scrolls had revealed some very surprising events which had been taking place thousands of years ago. The main part of the manuscript described in great detail the procedure for making a machine which defied gravity using just the earth's magnetism and solar energy. The earth was a rotating dynamo, which would induce potential energy triggered by the Sun's rays which would be converted into kinetic energy, by the special device causing the machine to levitate, move forward and backwards or sideways. The diagrams showed the exact construction of this special device which used no moving parts, but consisted of around a pound of 24K gold in five millimetre thick sheets supported by a frame of cylindrical-shaped pure iron rods placed at exact angles to form a pyramidal shape. There were other metals like copper, silver, and bronze in small quantities which were required to form the circuits, through which solar power would induce the energy. At the core of the pyramid was a perfect cube carved from a quartz crystal of specific nature. This machine was sufficient to power a small craft which could carry a payload of about 1,000 tons for a week, with only an hour of solar charge, leaving no emissions behind!

The chief sighed. He had the alternative to oil and gas reserves which were getting more and more expensive worldwide. But this would have to wait until his oil company was able to extract every drop of oil or gas, anywhere in the world. The investments made so far in infrastructures for removing the oil and gas from the bowels of the earth had to bring back as much profits as it could before he sprang the ultimate new power to the world and become the richest and most powerful man in the world! Hell, in the Universe! And that would also shut up the environmentalists with their eco-friendly cries! 'I must start buying up as much gold as I can, right away,' thought the chief. Of course, gold prices would shoot up. Now he understood why man since the beginning of history had always sought gold. It had now become a part of his DNA without knowing why he needed to acquire the golden metal! Somewhere along the timeline, man had forgotten to handover the ancient secrets. Well, he was glad they had. The future was now his alone.

He realised that Saddam hadn't lied when he claimed that he had the 'Mother of all Weapons'. He just hadn't known how to use it.

When Alan Rice entered his apartment that evening whistling a tune, he never knew what hit him. He was dead even before he collapsed on the floor. The 'gentleman' had been waiting for three hours in Alan's apartment. As he turned to leave the apartment, he picked up a canvas bag which contained a million dollars in cash. When he had broken into the apartment, he had quickly searched the entire place and had been surprised to find the bag containing a million dollars under the bed.

'Well,' he thought cheerfully as he took the elevator, 'maybe I should just tell the professor that this one is on the house.'

6

Miracles in Mumbai?

T HE CHANTING
PROCESSION of about
fifty people moved through the pouring rain on the heavily
flooded streets of Mumbai. On their shoulders, the four men
who were unknown to each other, carried a wooden frame
on which the dead body of a frail old man lay oblivious to
the downpour, covered with a white cotton sheet. Thunder
and lightning from the skies added to the mournful aura
of the group of people. It was nearing midnight, but even
this late, people were still walking on the roads trudging
their way home through the slush after office, stuck because
the local trains, which were the lifeline of Mumbai's
mass transport system, had been suspended due to the
tracks getting flooded. Traffic had come to a standstill
as the roads had become inundated with water. This was
probably the worst storm that Mumbai had ever witnessed

in its existence. It was two kilometres more to the funeral grounds, and the procession of mourners had already walked over twice that distance.

Hari Singh had been a cobbler and slept under the same street lamp, under which he worked by day. He considered himself to be a specialist, and this fact was generally acknowledged by all the people who had their shoes or chappals either mended or polished by him. Hari Singh had met the old man when he had wanted a pair of terribly worn-out footwear repaired. He had asked the young ten-year-old if he was interested in learning something which would help him in the future. Hari had said yes immediately and started visiting the old man every evening to be taught from a strange manuscript, which appeared to be ancient. Hari Singh had soon realised that he had to be educated to get a good job so as to make a decent living. He also found out that a decent academic education came with a price tag, so he started saving as much as a cobbler-cum-shoe shine boy could, outside the Victoria Terminus station in Mumbai. This he did by day and visited the old man who taught him to read and write, and then lectured from the strange scriptures every evening. Soon, he had saved enough money to start night school. While he was on the way to the school for procuring admission, he was caught by the beat constable, searched thoroughly, had his money confiscated, and then let go off with a threat and a smack to the head. This first but expensive lesson in economics changed the boy forever and so he decided to become rich so that no lousy constable could make off with his hard-earned money. He was wiry and thin, but he was determined to go to any length to achieve his dream. He attended the old man's discourses every evening, without fail. The old man had asked him about his school several times, but he had averted answering by saying that he would do so soon. While polishing shoes, Hari had regularly overheard people saying how they had made a killing at the stock market. He decided to try his hand at this game at the age of thirteen. The small savings from his work was invested by one of his customers who worked on the floor of the stock exchange and felt sympathy for the young lad. This first investment had given a three-fold return by evening. One-third of this was pocketed by the stock exchange man. Hari decided to study how the stock exchange actually worked and within a month had become completely familiar with the pattern. Fortune smiled upon the young boy, and within one year, he had quit his job as a cobbler; in five years, he had a car and a flat in the posh central suburbs of Mumbai. During this entire period, he continued to visit the old man every evening on weekdays, and while listening to the old man's lectures, continued to polish his shoes. That Tuesday evening on 26 July, he had intended to present the old man with a pair of new shoes that he had purchased from his profit on the exchange. When he reached the old man's house in the pouring rain, he found the neighbours leaving the house with sad tearful faces, who told him that the old man was no more. Hari Singh had rushed inside and seen that the attending doctor was packing up his things and was ready to leave. Hence, he was now part of the procession.

Gorakhbhai Tandel was a fisherman. He had started as a crew member of a fishing boat owned by another man named Tandel who was unrelated, bringing the daily haul of Pomfret, Surmai, and Bangda to the Ferry Wharf or Bhau-Cha-Dhakka near Dockyard Road, as it was popularly known. It was here, several years ago that he had met the old man on a Saturday morning, while he was sitting on the road side with a basket of fresh fish. The old man had purchased some fish from Gorakhbhai and had asked him if he was interested in learning something worthwhile. When the answer was yes, the old man had insisted that Gorakh should come to his home in South Mumbai whenever he had time and receive free discourses on the scriptures

from him. Gorakh had gone every morning after returning
from his fishing trip and listened to the old man's lectures,
which he would be asked to learn by heart and reproduce.
Every Saturday, Gorakh would personally carry selected
fish for the old man. Several years later, Gorakh married
the daughter of the fisherman Tandel and got the fishing
boat as his dowry. Over the years, he grew prosperous and
bought several fishing boats and stopped going out for
fishing, himself. Instead, he employed other fishermen to
gather the fish while he counted the money at home. He
continued visiting the old man every Saturday even after
becoming rich, bringing along the best fish for him. It was
monsoon season, so all fishermen had their boats tied up to
the wharf. That Tuesday morning, he had decided to carry
out a few repairs on his boats personally, which is why he
ended up near South Mumbai. Due to the incessant rain,
he found that no work could be done on the boats. On an
impulse, he decided to break tradition and went to see the
old man. When he managed to reach the old man's house,
he was grieved to see him already laid out on the wooden
frame and a holy man reading the last rites. He was also a
part of the procession.

Manav Kumar had been a school dropout. Crazed
with Bollywood fever, at the age of eighteen, he decided
to try his fortune in Mumbai. It was just by chance that as
he got off the train from Bhopal, he had been caught by
the ticket collector for travelling without a ticket. It so
happened that the old man, who was also waiting in line,
having returned from elsewhere had spoken to the TC and
paid the boy's fine. When Manav told the old man that he
was school dropout and had come to Mumbai to become
an actor, the old man had taken him home and had given
the boy a hot meal. He had asked him to come and attend
his discourses on the scriptures, whenever he could. He
promised and left the old man. Manav visited the old
man in the late evening every day for almost ten months

for learning the scriptures, while practically living on the benches in front of the Gateway of India, near the Taj Hotel. He went daily to a film studio in the suburb of Andheri, (without ticket, of course), and after those ten months, he miraculously got a minor role in a film. As years passed by, Manav finally became a star and his popularity soared, but he still managed to visit the old man once in a while. At the peak of his popularity, he had a brief spell with drugs and alcohol and then was hospitalised due to an overdose. After rehabilitation, he bounced back into the highest echelons of stardom. After this narrow escape, each day before going to bed, he promised himself that he would visit the old man, whose kindness had helped him since his very first day in Mumbai. It was just his bad luck that evening, while he was in South Mumbai that his car got stuck in a traffic jam that spread out over five kilometres. Through the rain splashing on his windscreen, he suddenly remembered that he was not far from the old man's house and decided to pay him a visit. He got down in the rain and asked his driver to drive on home without him, whenever the traffic cleared. When he reached the old man's home, he found that the old man had passed away, an hour ago. Manav stayed for the funeral.

As a small boy, Inspector Dhiraj Jadhav had worked as a waiter in a tiny roadside restaurant near Victoria Terminus. He would work from ten in the morning and finish at midnight every day. He would sleep on the premises. He earned a petty sum with breakfast, lunch, and dinner thrown in, which was nothing but the slop remaining from the day's pathetic menu. The day the old man had entered the restaurant and asked the boy if he was interested in studying, as he ate the oily samosas from the counter, was one Dhiraj would never forget. Dhiraj had taken up the old man's offer, and every day from seven to nine in the morning, he would study the scriptures under the old man's guidance. Although he had initially resisted, he had joined night school at the old man's insistence and had quit the restaurant by the time he turned twenty, having secured his secondary school certificate. During the period, when he was undergoing training to becoming a policeman, he managed to visit the old man occasionally. After diligent hard work over several years, he was finally promoted to the rank of sub-inspector. He visited the old man regularly, once he was transferred to Mumbai in Vikhroli. It was just by chance that on that Tuesday he happened to be present at the High Court in Southern Mumbai for giving evidence in a forgery case, when he thought of calling at the old man's house, after his case had been brought up before the judge. When he arrived at the house, he was shocked to know about the demise of the old man. He too was part of the crowd going to the funeral.

The rain was now coming down with a vengeance, causing pinpricks on the uncovered parts of the mourners. From the news being whispered, it appeared that the entire city of Mumbai was being inundated with the heaviest rainfall ever recorded in history. All street lights were off, and there were millions of people on the roads, trying to get to their homes, on foot, wading through the slush.

When the first few fellows, who were in front of the procession, suddenly found themselves in waist-deep water, they panicked and started retreating. The funeral procession had reached the suburb of Byculla, at a place where there was a steep dip in the road as it passed under a flyover. Due to the darkness, no one could see what lay under the bridge. There was a sudden confused pile up of the procession, and someone shouted that the road was blocked with deep water. The procession fell back, and the people in the procession started moving away. In the matter of a few minutes, all the people in the funeral procession departed, not making eye-to-eye contact with each other. This was as far as they were willing to go for an old man whom they barely knew as someone who stayed in their vicinity. Only the four young men carrying the wooden frame with the old man's body were left behind with their burden. The four, completely soaked to the skin, looked at each other, nodded when they saw the gleam of determination reflecting in each other's eyes and moved towards the flooded section of the road.

The water soon reached their waist, but they moved along without faltering, but cautiously. They carefully made their way through the flood waters, the two men in front feeling for any obstructions with their feet, before proceeding forwards. The water had now reached their shoulders, so that they had to hold the wooden frame high above their heads. They were still not halfway across and their thoughts were turning to doubt. Suddenly, one of them stumbled against an obstruction underwater. The others instinctively tightened their grip on the wooden frame, as they felt him stumble. Fortunately, he recovered his balance, as the others breathed a sigh of relief. Due to the sudden jerk, the old man's left leg rolled out from under the white sheet and struck the water. All of them heard the small splash that it made and turned to look at what had fallen in the water. As they saw the old man's leg touching the water, there was a sudden gurgling sound and the water started receding rapidly. In silent amazement, the four young men saw all the water around them disappear within minutes, until the bare road could be clearly seen. This was unbelievable! They had just seen an amazing spectacle! The four astonished men resumed their journey, after one of them had gently eased the old man's leg back on the frame. None of them spoke a word to each other, but each of them knew that he had been witness to nothing short of a miracle.

After an hour of traipsing through flooded streets, the four men reached the funeral grounds. They looked around but saw no one. Normally, there is always somebody present at the site to assist with the funeral, as well as to perform the last rites. It seemed that even the Gods had taken a break for those twenty-four hours, for the weather had become even more violent. The wind roared through the trees making a moaning sound, as if in grief. Lightning and thunder increased their display of strength. The four men gently laid down the wooden frame on top of a pile of twigs which was lying underneath a tin awning. They looked around for the man who performs the last rites and finally went in different directions to search for the man. Just when they were out of sight, the man whom they were looking for came out from the small structure which housed the toilet. When he saw the old man's body lying on the pile of twigs, he muttered under his breath. He hated people who wanted to get away from paying his dues for performing the last rites. This definitely looked like an abandoned body. Probably, this man's family was too poor, or perhaps it was an unidentified body, found on the streets of Mumbai. He moved up to the pile of twigs, on which lay the body of the old man, and commenced the last rites. He had just lit the pyre when he felt a strong burst of searing heat and a blinding flash of a powerful light in front of him, which was immediately followed by a deafening crack of thunder, which he did not hear. The lightning had struck him and instantly vaporised his body.

The loud explosion from the lightning alarmed the four men. They turned on their feet and ran back towards the place where they had left the old man. A shocking sight greeted them, which was beyond their imagination. The pile of twigs on which they had kept the wooden frame with the old man on it was ablaze! All of a sudden, the wind died down to a mild zephyr, and the rain reduced to a gentle drizzle as if to pay homage to the old man, while the four men joined their hands in silent prayer. It was the third miracle they had witnessed that day.

Two days later, workers from the Mumbai Municipal Corporation were on their rounds of the metropolis, clearing clogged drains on the streets of Mumbai. When their van reached Byculla, at the same spot where the road dipped under a flyover, they found that the manhole cover of the sewer system had been dislodged and was lying a few feet away from the opening. One of them marvelled at this fact and said this was possibly the only street which had not got flooded.

A small article was published in one of the daily newspapers in the 'missing persons' section. There was a photograph with a small note underneath, asking people to come forward and inform the police if they had sighted a man named Raghuram, who performed last rites and had gone missing from a funeral ground close to Byculla on the evening of 26 July.

Inspector Jadhav told me this story when I was travelling on a flight from Mumbai to Delhi. He said that he and the other three men believed that these were truly miracles. I did not have the heart to tell him the truth. It was obvious to me that he and his three friends were not keen on reading newspapers regularly. And of course, he did not know that I worked in the municipal corporation, in charge of the city drains.

7

Out of the Blue

*F*OR THE BENEFIT
of those who are not
familiar with Hindu mythology, there are Gods (Devas) and
Evil (Asuras). One of the Gods is Lord Yamadoot who is
the dedicated collector of human souls. He maintains the
balance of life and death on earth. He is also known to be
just in his decisions. Hence, it is he who decides whether a
soul should be liberated from rebirth, reborn in any form,
or sent to everlasting damnation, depending upon the
way the soul has lived, good, bad, or evil. To assist him in
coming to a correct decision, the enormous task of keeping
a record of deeds of the countless lives on earth, he has
an assistant called Chitragupt. Chitragupt's main role is
to maintain accurate records of each and every deed of
every soul on earth, which he then has to make available to
Yamadoot for deciding how a soul is to be dealt with. Once

a name has been entered in the Book, that person's clock starts ticking until his demise, which is ordained.

I have taken the liberty of some modification as to where Yamadoot assigns souls or how he monitors all deeds, but I am sure he will not mind as there is no malice intended, so neither should the reader.

As usual, Chitragupt had woken up early that day as well, and after getting ready, he had gone to his office, which was accessed through a door connected to his residence. At 8.30 a.m. when he sat down at his work desk, he realised that the Book of Records was not on his table. He was amazed. He was sure that he had left it right there last night, leaving his automatic recorder switched on. The automatic recorder was an integral part of the Book of Records and was solely used when he had to leave the room for any reason, including when he rested. Concerned that the Book could not be found on the desk, he quickly got up and started a frantic search of his office. While searching near his well-stocked library, he stumbled upon an obstruction and to his amazement found a broken piece of the automatic recorder at his feet, with most of its body lying under a cupboard. He exclaimed and bent down to pick up the broken equipment, while also taking a peek under the cupboard for his Book of Records. After a fruitless search, he cried out in frustration and pulled at his thinning hair. It was already 9.30 a.m. and he must present the Book of Records to Yamadoot, who would be waiting for him next door. He did not want to imagine what repercussions there would be at the loss of the Records, so he ran to open another door which connected his office to Yamadoot's court. He saw Yamadoot waiting impatiently on his golden throne with his chin cupped in his left hand, while the right hand fingers tapped feverishly on his knee. Chitragupt saw that the court was already filled with numerous souls standing in line, awaiting the verdict from Yamadoot.

'There you are! What's the matter, Chitragupt? You are late today. And why are you looking so upset?'

'Your Majesty! There has been a robbery. I cannot find the Book of Records.'

A stunned Yamadoot looked at Chitragupt with amazement which quickly turned to concern.

'Have you checked everywhere? Everyone knows that no one is allowed to enter my palace, be they Devas or Asuras, without my permission or they will perish immediately!'

'Your Majesty, I assure you that the Book is not in my office. I have searched everywhere. In fact, I found the broken pieces of the automatic recorder lying under one of my library cabinets. Surely, somebody has been fiddling around in my office.'

Yamadoot jumped up when he heard that the unique recorder was broken.

'What! Don't you know how valuable that automatic recorder is? It is just one of its kind and took several years to build and perfect!' roared the furious Yamadoot, as Chitragupt cringed under the force of anger from his boss and began to weep openly.

'Come, come. Stop crying. Let us go and search for the Book. I am sure we will find it lying about somewhere.'

Both of them entered Chitragupt's office, which looked like it had been ransacked. After a futile search, both of them went back, heavy-hearted and puzzled. Chitragupt kept wringing his hands nervously. Yamadoot sat silently on his throne and started thinking. He looked down at the broken automatic recorder in his hand and wondered who would have had the guts to do away with his Book. He looked up and saw with alarm that his entire court room was now filled almost to its peak capacity, with the lines of souls awaiting his decision. He had to think how he could solve this problem. He could not just casually send these souls to heaven or hell or be reborn, without accurate knowledge of the deeds of each soul. He was, after all, renowned for his sense of clean justice. 'I must think,' he told himself. Think, think . . .

*   *   *

Lord Brahma, the Creator of the Universe, woke up suddenly from his meditational trance and frowned. He had been disturbed by, what sounded to him, a crescendo of sounds of crying, screaming, praying, and moaning from people on earth. This had never happened before. Brahma's meditational trance was so powerful that only Lord Vishnu, the Preserver of Life, or Lord Shiva, the Destroyer of Evil, could penetrate his intense concentration and bring him out to reality. He was amazed at the strength of the pathetic sounds and tried to cover his ears to them keep out, without success. He immediately concentrated hard and called on Vishnu and Shiva to come to him. A few celestial minutes later, both the Lords came to Brahma with cotton balls in their ears. After courtesies were exchanged and all three of them were seated, Brahma said, 'I see that you both have been hearing the same thing that I have been hearing. What on earth is the matter with the people?'

'I think the population on earth has increased to astronomical proportions. Which is why we are hearing such loud prayers and wails,' said Vishnu. Brahma sat up and looked at Shiva.

'I agree. As the population has increased, so have people's problems. I must say that it is getting a tad difficult to entertain wishes and prayers of so many people all at once,' said Shiva.

'You are right. I have the same problem as well,' confirmed Vishnu.

'But why has the population suddenly shot up? Any ideas?'

They sat silently, pondering over the problem. At last Brahma sighed and looked at the other two.

'Let's call Yamadoot. May be he can shed some light on what has been happening.'

Shiva concentrated with his eyes closed and called upon Yamadoot to appear before them. Yamadoot immediately got up from his throne and walked down the stairs. He had been summoned. There was nothing else to think or do, but face the consequences. He shook himself into action and ordered Chitragupt to accompany him. Outside the palace door, they boarded Yamadoot's magnificent golden chariot, which was pulled by two huge coal black shiny bulls, and took off immediately for Brahmas' abode.

'Come in, come in, Yamadoot!' said Brahma. Yamadoot and Chitragupt entered and stood before the three Lords.

'Yamadoot, can you explain why the population on earth has shot up so much? I thought you were taking care of souls,' Brahma said. Yamadoot looked up, uncertain how he should explain what had gone wrong, while Chitragupt looked ready to burst into tears at any moment. All three Lords waited patiently for an explanation.

'My Lords, there has been a problem at my palace. We cannot find the Book of Records, which contains the details of each and every life and soul.'

The three Lords were stunned by this revelation. This was a calamity of monumental proportions! Never had any of them planned for a contingency such as this. Vishnu, the gentle-hearted, was the first to recover and asked softly, 'When did this happen?'

'My Lord, the loss came to light this morning. I and Chitragupt were discussing the best option on how to resume our work, without causing injustice to the souls waiting, when we got your summons,' replied Yamadoot, while Chitragupt quivered in the background.

'This morning? So that means that till now, fifty earth-years have passed,' stated Brahma, a little peeved at the delay in receiving this information. Yamadoot patiently explained what had transpired at his palace as well as in Chitragupt's office, which only caused all the three Lords to burn red with anger.

'How is it possible that the Book of Records is lost?' roared Shiva angrily. 'Who has dared to enter your palace in the heavens? I will annihilate them this instant!'

Chitragupt wailed at this statement and started pulling out his hair, as Yamadoot tried to console him.

'Calm down, son,' said Brahma, soothingly. He was worried. An uncontrolled population explosion on earth and a major backlog of souls awaiting judgment were huge problems. This required an immediate plan and urgent action. He looked at the other two Lords with the query clearly written on his bearded visage.

Vishnu spoke up, 'Lord Brahma, I suggest that we call an emergency meeting of all Devas and Asuras immediately. Have them search the heavens and the nether world, until they locate the Book.'

Shiva and Brahma nodded in agreement, while Yamadoot and Chitragupt looked on with relief on their faces.

The Devas and Asuras were immediately sent out instructions to search for the Book of Records. They were warned of the terrible consequences, should the Book not be found. Propelled into action, the Devas and Asuras commenced the search at once. It was several futile earth-months later that negative reports came in from both parties. The three Lords were now in an even more concerned state. There was nothing left for them to do other than cause a direct intervention into worldly affairs, by exterminating their entire creation. 'It would be such a pity,' they thought. Chitragupt wept when it dawned on him that somehow he was the cause, which would kill all humanity. Yamadoot too understood the enormity of such a decision and shook his head sorrowfully. It would be a pity to gather up and roll all the souls into one giant ball, just as it was at the beginning of time itself, and then start all over again. Just as each one of them was in deep contemplation as to how to proceed with the ghastly deed, Shiva spoke up with an exclamation. 'Wait! We still have not searched one place. Earth.'

Brahma, Vishnu, Yamadoot, and Chitragupt looked at him in surprise.

'What? Don't be so ridiculous! How can any human steal the Book? It is impossible!' scoffed Brahma.

Vishnu smiled and nodded as if in agreement with Shiva.

'Lord Brahma, what is the harm in searching? As it is, we are contemplating global destruction and complete annihilation, which is worse for humans than the predicament in which they find themselves at this time, and that too not of their own making. I fully agree with Lord Shiva. Let us send one of my Avatars to Earth and search for the Book. If lucky, we can go back to our meditation in peace,' he said. Brahma thought for a while before answering.

'OK, let's do it. But what Avatar will you take on this time?' queried Brahma.

'Well, looking at the colossal amount of corruption on earth, a very rich man, I think, will be able to bribe his way and get results quicker than any other Avatar of mine.'

'So be it. But there has to be a deadline for this search. We cannot allow letting humanity suffer as they are now. I feel one earth-month is all I can sanction for this venture, after which we will proceed to carry out what we have all thought about sub-consciously,' said Brahma with a shudder.

So it was agreed that Vishnu's 'rich man' Avatar would proceed to earth immediately.

*   *   *

The Avatar, who went by the name of Mr Krishnan, searched high and low everywhere, browsing through all continents, using teleportation to save on travelling time, but the missing Book still remained elusive. He had spent every penny that he had carried with him and was down to his last few coins. Tired, hungry, and now wearing tattered clothes unfit even for a beggar, he walked towards the last city which remained to be searched. His eyes were bloodshot, and his shoes had more holes than leather. He had run out of time. All that remained were the last twenty-four hours of earth time of the thirty days sanctioned by Brahma. As he walked onwards, he spied a dusty road leading into the brush on his right, which looked like a short cut to the last town on his list. He was glad to finally walk, as the constant zipping about had drained him of his energy. After a few miles down the dusty path, he saw a small broken down house at the base of a small hillock on his right, with smoke coming out from one of the doorways. An aroma of fresh food being cooked wafted towards the weary man, which set his empty stomach growling. He dragged himself hurriedly towards the dilapidated structure and knocked on the open front door. A middle-aged man of average height, but woefully thin, came out. He looked curiously at the man in front of him, and his expression softened when he saw the pitiful state he was in. He took the stranger by the shoulder and guided him inside the cool shade of his house.

'Come in, stranger. You appear to be all in. Take a seat and relax while I fetch you some water.'

Krishnan sat down gratefully on the only chair in the room. On the far side of the room was a cot sparsely covered with a torn and stained bed sheet, barely hiding the old and battered mattress, on which lay an old man, apparently asleep. He took a look around the room and saw the poverty in which these people lived. He saw the door through which the man had entered and was sure that it was the kitchen, as the smell of food was much stronger now. The man of the house came out with a steel tumbler and a discoloured plastic water jug that had seen cleaner days once upon a time. He drank the tepid water gratefully and eased his parched throat.

'Thank you,' said Krishnan. The man bowed in acknowledgement.

'You are my guest. This was the least I could do. Where are you headed, my friend?'

'I am going to the next town. I thought this was a short cut, but is apparently not.'

'Do you work or live there?' queried the man.

'Neither. I am actually searching for something, and I believe it is close by, so I guessed that the town would be the most likely place where I could find it,' Krishnan said.

'Well, it is almost lunch time, and I am sure that you are hungry, so let us eat. My wife has just made food,' said the man. Krishnan nodded and thanked the man for his hospitality. The man went inside, and within a few minutes came out with two plates, loaded with a pitiful helping of rice, vegetable curry, and a woeful onion.

The two of them sat down on the floor, and Krishnan immediately attacked the food, ravenously. Seeing that his meal was over, the man told him to go inside the kitchen where he would find a basin to wash his hands.

Krishnan entered the kitchen, washed his hands, and thanked the man's wife for the meal. She smiled at him from where she sat in one corner of the kitchen, a frail and small woman. A boy, about five years old, sat in front of her with his back towards him, talking to himself, while he bent over whatever he was doing. The boy stopped talking when he heard the stranger's voice and turned around to look at him. In his hand, he held a pen. The stranger asked him if he was studying, which was responded to by a nod from the boy. When Krishnan walked towards the child to see what he had been scribbling, he got a shock. The boy had apparently been scribbling in what he knew was the Book of Records! He cried out in excitement, which scared the boy and his mother, while the alarmed husband came running into the kitchen.

'Where did you find this book?' exclaimed Krishnan, trembling with excitement. 'This is what I have been looking for!'

The husband looked at the stranger curiously, wondering if he had invited a mad man into his house.

'First, tell me why you have been looking for this book? What is it to you?' queried the man in response. Krishnan could not take his eyes off the Book. Reluctantly, he looked at the man and thought fast. He had to come up with a convincing story or else get into a fight with him, which did not appeal to him.

'I will tell you everything. The company that I work for maintains a detailed record of financial—and product-related transactions in this Book. It is too complicated to explain in detail, but the gist of the matter is that some of our employees misplaced it. This caused a huge backlog of work and financial loss to the Company. I had been directed by my boss to find this Book, or lose my job. You must let me take it back.'

The husband was silent for a few moments as he took in this information. The delight and relief on the stranger's face appeared to be genuine. He made up his mind instantly.

'I am glad that you have found what you were looking for. Of course, you can have it back.'

'Where did you find it?' Krishnan asked.

The man laughed bitterly.

'You must ask my father who will explain everything to you,' said the man.

They went to the front room. The man woke up the old man on the cot, who was his father. He whispered something in his ear, and the old man suddenly became alert and nodded.

'Come closer, stranger. I am afraid my voice is not as strong as it was in my youth,' he said in a quavering voice.

Krishnan sat down at the edge of the cot, close to the old man.

'My luck turned for the worse about fifty years back. I was a happy man with a steady job, a house in the city, and a good income. My son was studying in the best school in town. I bought this piece of land at that time as investment, since it is not far from the city. One weekend, the three of us came out here for a picnic and also to plan how we would improve the interiors of the house. We sat down in this now broken-down house, which was already on the property when I purchased it. As we sat down to enjoy our picnic basket, we heard an explosion outside that shook the house. We immediately ran out to see what was happening. You see that small hillock? A cloud of dust appeared from behind it. As the hillock is at the edge of my property, I thought it was somebody using my land for mining or some illegal purpose. I told my family to wait near the house and went across the hillock to investigate. A very curious sight met my eyes. There, behind the hillock was a newly formed crater from which dust was still billowing. I made my way down the hill and slowly went into the crater, which was about six feet deep and about ten feet across. That is when I saw this book, lying in the crater. I looked all around, but could see nobody. It was just as if the book had dropped from the sky. The book was too heavy for me to pick up, so I dragged it all the way into this room. I opened it to try and figure out who it belonged to but found that the book was written in a strange language, so I just left the book here,' said the old man. He wheezed, as if out of breath.

'If you were well-off, then how are you in this position now?'

The old man smiled bitterly, remembering his happier days.

'Well, stranger, do you believe in fate? This damn book was what caused all our miseries, I feel. I and my late wife were puzzled at the sudden appearance of this book and discussed it at length but could find no explanation. We even thought of contacting the police, but I knew they would laugh at us. Anyhow, by evening, we were on our way home, talking about the curious incident that we had witnessed. When we reached the corner of our street, there appeared to be a lot of commotion. Police and fire brigade tenders were attending to a fire on our street. It turned out to be our house which was blazing. There was nothing remaining by the time the fire was extinguished. The entire house was gutted along with our belongings. We shifted to a hotel for a couple of days. Then within a month, the company that I worked for, closed down. I sold the land that my burnt house stood on and got a meagre amount for it. I tried very hard to get another job, but with the state of the economy, downsizing of companies and inflation, I was unsuccessful. Finally, we decided to shift here, as this was the only place we could go to. My savings have been depleting slowly ever since, hence we now live in extreme poverty. When we first shifted here and I saw this book again, I was enraged and tried to tear the pages. I even tried burning the book, but it seems to be made of a strange material, which does not tear or even burn.'

Krishnan shivered when he heard that the man had tried to destroy the Book. He picked up the Book with a grunt, straining his muscles. Having heard the story, he was moved by compassion. Turning to the old man, he said, 'Sir, I thank you and your son, for taking care of this Book. Yes, you are correct. It is written in an ancient language so that if this landed in the hands of any rival company, they could not make sense of what has been recorded. Now, with your kind permission, please allow me to take this Book back to where it belongs, as my Company officials are anxiously waiting for it.'

The old man nodded and asked, 'Will you do me one favour?'

'Sure sir, anything you want. You have done a huge favour to me by keeping the book safe.'

'I am so sorry to ask,' said the old man, appearing extremely embarrassed. Hell! He had actually tried to burn the damn book.

Krishnan knew that this was a proud old man and was too embarrassed to ask for favours.

'Go ahead, sir, ask away. I will be more than pleased to help you.'

'All right, can you possibly find a job for my son in your Company? Any job will do. He is a hard worker and will not let you or the Company down. Alas, he could not complete his education due to my financial downfall.'

Krishnan was astounded at this request. He knew that as one of the three mighty Lords, he could not back out of this situation. He had to grant this old man's wishes.

'I cannot promise, but let me see what I can do once I get back,' Krishnan said gently.

The old man and his son thanked him and asked if he wanted to rest. He thanked them for their hospitality, but said that he had to return immediately. He shook hands with the old man, his son, and the little boy. Taking his leave, Krishnan walked away, carrying the heavy Book of Records on his shoulders, as the family waved goodbye to him. As soon as the house was out of sight, the Avatar immediately concentrated hard and teleported back to the Abode of the Lords.

* * *

The moment Vishnu entered, he found Brahma, Shiva, Yamadoot, and Chitragupt eagerly waiting for him. At the sight of the Book on his shoulders, Chitragupt cried out in glee and ran eagerly towards Vishnu. He smiled at Chitragupt and handed over the Book of Records to him.

'Well, it appears that you have been successful in your venture. Where did you find it?' queried Brahma, pleased with the outcome.

Shiva and Yamadoot congratulated him as well. Vishnu took a seat and recited all that he had experienced and finally asked, 'So do we know how this Book landed up on earth?'

Yamadoot answered 'My Lord, after you left, we carried out a thorough investigation and found that the Book, which Chitragupt normally keeps on his desk was blown off due to a strong gust of wind which blew in from the open window. Unfortunately, the portal through which Chitragupt studies deeds of all souls lies directly below the left-hand edge of the table. Actually, the portal does not allow even thoughts or light to pass through it towards earth. Just because the Book of Records is a blessed object, the portal allowed it to pass through and head towards earth.'

Vishnu nodded in understanding.

'OK, but now, there is a small problem. The man requested me to find a suitable position for him in the "Company" that I supposedly work for. What are we going to do about that?'

Shiva frowned. He was slightly bugged that another problem had cropped up. Meanwhile, after being directed by his Master, Chitragupt flicked through the pages of the Book of Records to see where he had left off his work. Upon reaching the last page, he cried out loudly, moaned, and fell to the floor in a dead faint in front of the four amazed Gods, the Book landing with an enormous thud.

Yamadoot leaped to Chitragupt's side and held him up in a sitting position, while Brahma immediately used a small amount of elixir to revive him. Shiva picked up the Book of Records from the floor, assisted by Vishnu. Curiosity caused them to examine what Chitragupt had read, which had caused him to faint. They flicked through until they reached the page where various animals had been drawn and several names had been written in a scrawling, untidy handwriting, as if done by a child of four or five.

Their faces turned white, and they almost dropped the book as well. Brahma saw their expression and asked them what the matter was. When he got no reply, he impatiently got up and grabbed the Book from their hands and read what was written.

The entries, scribbled in a juvenile hand, in the left-hand column were as follows;

Anand
Jeevan
Jyoti
Ayush

Which were the names of the poor old man, his middle-aged son, his daughter-in-law, and his five-year-old grandson.

Under these names were three other names;

Brahma
Vishnu
Shiva

The three Gods, the family prayed to.

8

For Want of a Nail...

I HAD JUST CHECKED into a hotel in the Sardinian port of Cagliari when my cell phone started ringing. The call was from the port agent, advising me that due to inclement weather conditions, my flight to Rome had been rescheduled for the afternoon of the day after tomorrow and all going well, he would pick me up at 10 a.m. I acknowledged this piece of unpleasant information, although, given the weather conditions, it wasn't exactly surprising. I told him that I would be ready at the stated time and day. It is always a bad omen when one is delayed indefinitely, especially when going on vacation.

There had been severe weather conditions in the central Mediterranean Sea that December, as I brought my ship alongside the general cargo berth. Although the Mediterranean Sea is relatively enclosed and cocooned, winter weather in these parts can get very nasty. The central and eastern portion of this sea can be especially terrible in the winter season. I had disembarked from my ship that bleak day in December, welcomed by a strong breeze which may sound to a landlubber to be a pleasant wind, but which in nautical terms is actually quite severe. When the ambient temperature is low and there is a strong wind blowing, it is the wind-chill factor that gets to you.

My last command was on an old, general cargo ship which was on a tramp run. The owners had decided to run her wherever they could get legitimate cargo for their forty-year-old rust bucket. I had started my career as a deck apprentice on board the same vessel, twenty-two years ago. After the rigmarole of securing certificates of competency at regular intervals for the appropriate ranks, I had finally accomplished the final frontier of commanding my own ship at the age of thirty-five. After five years in command, I was now, already rated as a senior master. Curiously the *San Bonito*, as she was called, and I were born in the same month and year.

There had been no doubt in my mind when I had been asked by my father, what field I wanted to pursue to be able to make an honest living, after I had passed my Higher Secondary Certificate. The results were not astounding, but a decent score of about 80 per cent, which meant a lot in that era, decided my outcome. Unhesitatingly, I had told him of my dream to pursue the family tradition of putting out to sea. My father appeared immensely pleased, and this was immediately agreed upon. The initial days of training now seem like a blur. The camaraderie, oaths of un-meaningful pacts, and the occasional punishment for stepping out of discipline remain just a fond memory. When we are younger, things always appear in black or white. It's only when one has experienced the harshness of life that one realises the futility of fighting it all, as no school in the world trains you for handling grey areas, of which life is mostly made up of.

The miniscule hotel room was filled with a single bed, a small writing table, a chair, and a tiny bathroom. An ancient fifteen-inch television set stood as majestically as it could, on a tiny dressing table, demanding attention as the only electronic appliance, other than the lights and the table fan. A lonely fly had been ushered in to keep me company. Having shaved and showered, I decided to take a stroll around the old beaten pathways leading up to the older parts of Cagliari. Although it was just 7 p.m., it was already pitch-dark outside. I climbed up the cobblestoned lanes winding uphill, as the cold wind gusted around me. There were hardly any tourists at this time of the year, most preferring the warmer climates of the tropics. After almost an hour of traipsing around, I was eager to get out of the savage wind. I pulled up the collar of my leather jacket and entered a restaurant which proclaimed the name 'Ristorante Spensierato' or the Happy-go-lucky restaurant. When I entered the dimly lit premises, there was nobody inside except for a massive figure, which sat with a forlorn and doleful look behind a table in the far corner.

'Good evening,' I said, as I walked in. The gentleman, who as I later learnt, was the landlord of the inn, got up with a wide smile on his fat moon-face, and wished me heartily with a 'Buona sera, signore' with genuine warmth, which displayed his happiness to see company on such a god-forsaken evening.

'Come, come, my friend. Please seet near fire. Ees molto freddo, is not so?' he queried.

I acknowledged. The landlord was a man of ample girth, more than six feet tall and about fifty-five years old. I sat down at a table close to the fireplace, toasting my freezing hands. An Italian opera was playing on the radio by the main counter. The landlord presented the menu card to me with a flourish. I decided on a glass of house wine and a sausage and vegetable stew. The landlord went away with my order. As I sat there looking around me, I noticed that the restaurant appeared to be very old and probably had been used for a different purpose in another era. There were a few faded paintings hanging on the walls. Lampshades adorned the place but threw minimal light around, due to the sooty and grimy glass. My host returned with a basket of warm bread and the glass of house wine.

'You like wine, my friend?'

'Occasionally, yes,' I said.

'Wine is very good for you, signore. It keeps the heart young and strong,' he said in a whisper, as if parting with a deadly secret.

'I am sure you are right,' I said and smiled at this sagacious piece of well-known information, as I took a sip.

'Excellent! I wonder why the wine has a woody flavour,' I remarked. It was definitely a very different wine from what I had occasionally taken on board.

'Do you wanna see the place where we store the house wine?' he asked eagerly.

'Sure, if you don't mind.'

He led me to the other end inside the restaurant, where he picked up an ancient chain attached to a wooden hatch which fitted over a rectangular opening in the floor. He proceeded down stone steps with a hand-lamp in his hand and beckoned me to follow him. The damp and gloomy interior of the stone-walled room was filled with the smell of ageing wood accompanied with the sweet-sour smell of fermented grapes, there being hardly any visible ventilation. There were three huge wooden casks in the middle of the room, which took up almost all the space.

'The first cask, signore, is filled with wine from grapes picked in 1997. We had a very good harvest that year in Sardinia,' said my host genially.

Knowing a bit about wines, I proceeded to ask him which fruit had been responsible for the contents of the cask from which I was indulging in.

'The wine that you have comes from the third cask. It is a fruit which I harvest myself and brew. It is grown on ten acres of my ancestral marshland. The grapes picked are from the year 2000. Even I was surprised with the fruit at that time as it was deep red and so heavy with nectar that they were falling off the trees by themselves! I had thought them to be overburdened with water, but it turned out to be a unique and concentrated fruit! Over here in Sardinia, we have grape varieties which come from Bovale species: Bovale Sardo, Bovale Mannu, and Bovale of Spain. The wine is produced in a lot of communes in Cagliari's province, and before receiving the D.O.C, it used to be exported to the whole of Italy and France as blending wine,' educated the landlord. 'But seriously, now we have molto competition from the other grape-growing nations. Ah, but still we have the best vino and olives in the world,' he said proudly.

My tour and lessons over, we turned back to go up to the restaurant where my glass of wine awaited me.

'I see your meal is ready, signore,' he said. He walked up to the food counter, behind which I could make out two hands doling out a steamy brew of stew from a pot into a large porcelain bowl. When the landlord brought over my meal, I saw that there was a dish filled with celery, olives, and sliced tomato on the side. A bottle of extra-virgin olive oil was already on the table. As I started digging into my salad with gusto, the landlord asked me, 'So what do you do, signore, in Cagliari?'

'I just disembarked from a ship. I was the captain of the MV *San Bonito*. Now on my way home to have a vacation,' I said.

'Oh my God, you are a capitano! E bene! I am honoured by your visit to my humble restaurant, signore capitano! Please, I am deeply pleased to have you here,' said my host, beaming widely.

'Allow me to introduce myself, I am Giuseppe Moretti, yes,' he said and bowed low while introducing himself. 'Quite a decent and bumbling old gentleman,' I thought to myself. 'I am so deeply honoured that you should come to my humble restorante, rather than calling at some of the big and popular ones. Grazie, signore.'

I felt embarrassed to see him in this fashion. All evidences pointed to the fact that this man had not been getting good business for a long time. I sincerely felt bad for the poor man. His entire appearance was that of a man without much activity and not doing too well in life. His stained white shirt and worn-out dark brown trousers were very much a reflection of the state of his restaurant.

My host said, 'I remember going out fishing with my grandfather when I was a little boy. It used to be a great experience for me. But that was a very long time ago. So tell me, which countries have you been to so far, signore capitano?'

I have had this question thrown at me innumerable times and replied, 'Well, all countries in the Mediterranean region, USA, all countries on both the coasts of South America, Caribbean, all countries in the Far East and Persian Gulf and Australia.'

Giuseppe gazed at me as reverently, as if he had seen the Pope himself.

'You signore, are lucky. Most of us simple folks here on Sardinia, only see Sardinia for their entire life. I myself have never travelled outside, other than a few trips to Roma. You are indeed a lucky man,' said Giuseppe. 'Are you married, capitano?'

'Not yet,' I said.

'Ah, you have not yet found the femme fatale, eh?' he queried, with a twinkle in his eye, and chuckled.

'Escusi but, how old are you, signore, 35-36?' he asked.

'Actually, I am forty,' I said feeling a bit happier that I could still pass as someone five years younger.

'You are remarkably fit, signore. I compliment you,' he said.

'Thank you.'

After an hour of chit-chatting with Giuseppe and another glass of wine, I asked how much I owed him. He refused to charge me for the wine, or take a tip in spite of my persistence, so around 9 p.m., I left, after wishing him a good night, to return to my humble hotel room.

Lights from restaurants along the street were already being switched off, leaving only small yellow street lamps on. As I made my way down the dark cobblestone pathway, a light mist swirled around the dull street lamps. There was nobody walking around on the streets, as far as I could see. The wind force had increased, and the temperature had dropped significantly. The moon peaked out occasionally from behind dark clouds in the dreary night sky. As I turned a corner about 100 metres from my motel, a sudden blackout occurred. It was a second before I realised that it wasn't the lights. Somebody had thrown a black hood over my head and had grabbed me around the shoulders, pushing me forcefully along. Reflexively, while trying to turn around, I hit out left and right and felt my right connect with something bony, which gave a sharp crack. The loud howl from my attacker pleased me immensely. I have had my share of barroom brawls in younger days, although always ended up on the losing side. As I continued to hurl my fists around me, something heavy struck me on the head. My losing streak was intact, as I fell unconscious to the ground.

When I returned to consciousness, I had a pounding pain at the back of my head, and my eyesight was blurred. The first thing that I became aware of was that the whole place seemed to be heaving up and down. Maybe it was the effect of the terrible blow to my head. It was a few minutes later that I recognised that the movement was similar to that felt in a boat or a small ship, when tied up alongside a wharf and there is a swell in the harbour. I also realised that it was extremely cold as I lay shivering on what felt like a coiled mooring rope used on ships. My sight had still not returned fully, but I could make out the lights around me through the black shroud, which was around my head. The wail of the gusting wind and the dull throb of pounding blood in my head and ears from the whack on my head were the only sounds that I could hear. My hands appeared to have been tied, as were my feet. As I tried to wriggle my hands free, the knots only got tighter which meant that they were done professionally by a sailor or more likely, a fisherman. It is a curious fact, but now-a-days, not many sailors can boast of being able to tie all the knots, which were the basics of seamanship in my days as a Cadet. I found that just trying to sit up, increased the throbbing in my head. I felt angry at my predicament and swore softly. I had no clue who had kidnapped me and why. I had barely kept a hundred Euros in my wallet along with two credit cards, and the wrist watch was a cheap Casio, which could be bought anywhere in the world. After trying to free myself, I gave up and tried to take deep breaths to clear my brain. The next thing was the overpowering smell. The place in which I was trussed up reeked of fish. So this was most likely a fishing boat or a trawler.

I heard something and held my breath, which was coming in rasps, to try and listen carefully. Footsteps of at least two or three persons were getting louder as they approached. Someone coughed and spoke something which was muffled. I strained my eyes to see through the black veil, but gave up. There was nothing I could do at this moment. My watch suddenly beeped twice in rapid succession, which meant that it was either ten, eleven, midnight, or later. I had no clue how long I had been unconscious. I decided to keep as quiet as possible and try to learn as much as I could from the voices outside. There was a crane operating somewhere on board, as I heard the familiar sound of a winch working in the background. After sometime, a jarring thud from somewhere was followed by an angry retort. Probably the crane operator was getting an earful for not being careful with whatever was being loaded. A pair of footsteps approached where I was lying and a badly maintained door creaked open accompanied by a rush of wind. My teeth immediately started chattering due to the cold wind. I peered through my hood trying to get a glimpse of who had captured me, without success.

'Who are you and what the hell is going on?' I shouted.

The only answer I got was a blow which landed on my left ear sending bells ringing and flashes exploding in my vision. I almost lost consciousness again and shook my head to clear the ringing. The silent one retreated and slammed the door shut behind him. I grimaced with the pain at the back of my head and my left ear which now felt as if it was burning. There were voices again outside my door, and the door opened once again. I tensed myself for another punch. Someone spoke in Italian, and I was whisked upright to a standing position. The ropes tying my legs were removed, and I could feel blood pounding into the soles of my feet, after having been released from captivity of the tight knots. I felt a large hand at the back of my neck pushing me towards what I estimated was the door and guided me ahead. There was a sudden and uncomfortable pain in my side, which felt like the unpleasant end of a gun. My body reflexively stiffened, knowing what a bullet wound from close range could do to a man.

It was 1996, and I was a Second Mate then and also the dedicated medical officer on board. We were transiting the Sunda Straits off Indonesia. Around midnight, pirates had boarded our ship and taken the Master hostage at gunpoint. The Master was a red-blooded Irishman and had fought back, only to be shot point-blank in the stomach. The fact that he survived had nothing to do with the acumen of my treatment, but his own hardihood. The burns from the gun being fired so close to the body, the blood and entrails hanging out, and the large exit wound had haunted me for several months.

I was led up a flight of stairs, which I identified as the companionway outside the superstructure. The wind was now blowing fiercely and had turned into a strong gale. On the way up, I counted the steps and the decks, until I heard the familiar sound of the bridge wing door sliding open. No other door in the world sounds like this. Once inside, I was pushed onto a sofa. The smell of hot coffee was overpowering. The hood over my head was suddenly pulled off. There were no lights on the bridge except for the loom of light coming from what looked like a chart table. There were at least three figures moving around in the semi-darkness. A dark shape moved towards me with a knife. I recoiled instinctively, but there was not much space on the sofa, as I had two men sitting on either side. My arms were held by the two at my side forcing my hands up towards the guy with the knife. The knife moved with a glint and cut the rope tying my hands. It must have been a very sharp knife as the rope was a 14-mm wet manila rope. I was then thrust into a standing position.

'Good evening, capitano,' said a deep voice from the chart table, but I could see nothing, as the chart table light was facing down and pointed towards my side. 'I trust that you will not make a fuss or try to fight your way out. We don't want to waste time and would appreciate your cooperation. For your information, we have two men standing guard with guns at each deck level and four men armed similarly at the gangway hidden in the shadows.'

That sounded like overkill to me as I had no intention of trying to break my way out with the two heavily built thugs on both my sides. I peered towards the chart table trying to pierce the darkness but could see nothing other than a reflection from the far side bridge windows. Outside, gale force winds howled and the boat rolled and creaked, surging along the berth, struggling desperately against her moorings. I decided that silence was the best way to deal with this situation. The pounding in my head had now reduced to an unpleasant throb, with a gentle uneven rhythm.

'Get him here,' commanded the same voice from the far side. I was pushed towards the chart table. In the dim light, I saw a tall, thin man. He thrust out his hand. As I automatically reached out to shake hands, something caught my attention. A badly healed scar! Where had I seen it before? I knew I had seen it somewhere recently but could not place it. Before I knew it, I was shaking hands with the man. I glanced at a clock on the chart table. It was 10.15 p.m.

'Welcome, captain. My apologies for the rough way you were handled, but we would not have taken "no" for an answer, so this was the only way. 100 per cent guaranteed. Give him a cup of coffee, Carlos,' he said.

One of the men brought me a mug full of hot, steaming black coffee. I accepted the mug and took a sip.

'Sit down, captain,' said the same man who appeared to be in charge. I did as bid and sat down in a chair near the chart table. 'I am glad that you are being cooperative and have not asked any questions so far.'

'May I at least know what the hell is going on? Who the hell are you people, and what do you want from me?' I demanded hotly. My two bodyguards moved up towards me menacingly, as if to punch me out of existence but were stopped by a sharp retort from their leader. He spoke something rapidly in Italian, and few of the men left the bridge, leaving only myself, the man with the scar on his hand, and two men whom I still could not see properly in the darkness.

'Captain, I have a proposition for you. I want you to take this trawler with me and some of my friends, wherever I tell you to, without any questions. If you do exactly as I say, you will be rewarded with 25,000 US dollars. I would not recommend you to say no, as then there will be no other option left to us but to kill you. And don't think anyone will notice your absence, well, at least for two days. We know that you have a flight on Sunday at 10 a.m.,' said Scar-hand.

'Listen, I do not want anything from you. Just tell me what help you want and I will do it if I can,' I said, not wanting to get into another round of destroying my looks or as the man promised, ensuring a funeral in which I would play the leading part.

'Good. I am pleased that you are agreeable. Your reward will be paid to you, my word on it. Come here, capitano. Take a look at this chart carefully. I want you to take me and my men to this rock called Pollastro, marked here to pick up a few . . . ummm . . . passengers and baggage. You do not have to bother with them. They will be my guests and responsibility. Then you will plot a course for Gibraltar, where we will refuel. I will give you further instructions at a later stage.'

'Look, mate, this is a simple thing! Any experienced fisherman or an Able Seaman can get you to wherever you want. It doesn't need my input,' I said. Scar-hand nodded at one of the men in the shadows, standing behind me, and he moved in and hit me in my kidneys. Pain exploded in my lower back, and I collapsed on the deck. After a few minutes, I was able to gasp for breath and started to sit up when a kick landed on the same spot, and I passed out due to the pain. I felt cold water being splashed on my face as I came back to consciousness. The pain in my side and back was excruciating.

'OK, capitano. Now you know that there is no way out for you. Like I said before, just cooperate with us completely and you will have no problems,' snarled

Scar-hand. I could not respond, other than nodding my head. I decided to go along with whatever he wanted. The two men picked me up, dragged me to the couch, and I was left alone, while the three discussed something in whispers. After a few minutes, I felt much better, although my head and back were still throbbing. The crane on deck had stopped its work.

I got on my feet and went to the chart table. The three men immediately stopped talking, and Scar-hand came towards me. I looked at the torn and smudged British Admiralty chart and commenced plotting rhumb line courses to a spot marked with a red circle, which surrounded the three rocks known as Galitons de l'est or 'The Dogs', just about one nautical mile north of the main central Galite Island. Scar-hand had mentioned that he wanted me to take him to the middle rock known as Pollastro, which was situated between the rocks called Gallo to the north and Gallina to the south. The distance from Cape Spartivento in the south of Sardinia to our destination was about eighty nautical miles. The Galite Islands or Jazirat Jalitah in Arabic are a rocky group of islands of volcanic origin that belong to Bizerte Governorate of northern Tunisia. They are located about twenty nautical miles northwest of Cape Serrat, the closest point of the Tunisian mainland coast. The Galite Channel separates the two. About forty-six nautical miles to the SSW of the Galite Islands lies the city of Tabarka on the mainland. The islands of the group sit atop Banc de Galite. I wondered what Scar-hand and his friends were up to. The approach to the middle rock, known as Pollastro, was not exactly difficult for a trawler of this size, but given the weather conditions, I was certain that it would take some skilful ship-handling on my part. Scar-hand had been observing what I was doing and finally nodded in agreement.

'Good. Now let's get underway,' he said to me, and turning to the two men with him, he told one of them in Italian to go down and tell the crew to cast off. Within fifteen minutes, we had slipped our moorings and were underway, rolling and pitching heavily in the surging swell inside the harbour. I had taken the wheel myself, which on ships, is normally done by an Able Seaman. There is huge difference in handling a ship of 10,000 tons and handling a trawler of seventy-five tons, especially in rough weather. This trawler had a powerful Mitsubishi engine which gave me 2,000 horsepower to work with. I manoeuvred the trawler gently until we turned around to a southerly heading. The wind blew in from the west at gale force, causing a three-metre swell outside the breakwater. I had decided to remain in the lee of the island until we reached Capo Spartivento, which was about twenty-five nautical miles to the south-west. This would give us relatively calmer waters, which would allow us to make good speed.

On the sparsely equipped navigation bridge, with me were Scar-hand and his two men. I presumed that the others were somewhere in the accommodation or in the tiny engine room, as the swell and waves, which regularly crashed over the trawlers decks, meant immediate death for any man. I had briefly counted at least seven men on deck at the beginning, which meant that including Scar-hand, there were at least nine others. The short 105-nautical mile voyage would take us about eight hours in this weather. When we were clear of Capo Spartivento, the full effect of the swell, wind, and rain caught us. Keeping the heading at 195 on the magnetic compass was out of the question, so I ended up steering between 175 and 215. Occasionally, one of Scar-hand's men would come and relieve me on the wheel for me to plot our position using a hand-held GPS, which had been handed over to me by one of the men. Each time that I plotted a position, Scar-hand would come and scrutinise what I had done.

It was no surprise that there were no other boats at sea, except for the regular traffic of merchant ships, headed either for Port Said for their Suez Canal transit, or those bound for Europe, headed towards the Straits of Gibraltar. The next six hours were the most tiring ones of my life, and my arms ached from the constant steering.

We had surprisingly made good speed. When we were finally about 200 meters from the Gallo rock, Scar-hand told me to stop the engine. An hour earlier, he had left the bridge for about fifteen minutes, after which a few of his men had gone out on deck. Outside, it was pitch dark, but the weather had subsided to force 6. I heaved to and kept the engine throttled at minimum speed astern to slow her down. It was 05.30 a.m. The two men with Scar-hand left the bridge and made their way down to the fore deck.

'Well done, capitano,' complimented Scar-hand, as he handed me a cup of black steaming coffee, 'So far you have done a good job. I hope for your sake that you will continue to do so. Go ahead and ask what you will.'

I pondered over this last statement, remembering the kick in my kidneys, when I had last opened my mouth. Scar-hand had a gun stuck into his belt. Still, curiosity got the better of me as I took a big sip from my coffee mug.

'What exactly is happening here? Who are you people, and why am I helping you?'

Scar-hand nodded.

'You do deserve to know a bit of what is happening and what the next step is going to be. OK, listen carefully now. We had to take your help as our capitano was injured when we were loading some crates, earlier last evening, before we picked you up. Believe me, you were God-sent for us. We are presently waiting for some people who will be coming from Tunisia. Pollastro rock is our rendezvous point. My men will take three inflatable Zodiacs to pick them up. Once they join us, we will head towards Gibraltar Straits. Fifty miles before the straits, off the coast of

Morocco, we will rendezvous with another trawler which will refuel us. She will be carrying another captain, who is employed by these people who are joining us. Then all of us, including you, will transfer to the refuelling ship and head back to Cagliari. The people who are joining us shortly will be taking the boat to wherever they want. That is not our concern. Once we are back in Cagliari, you will be free to go wherever you want,' said Scar-hand. I heard this information in silence. It was a certainty that these Italians were into human-trafficking. I had heard about such things before and read about it in newspapers but had never expected to be a part of it.

'What about the crates that were loaded? What's in those? And who are these people whom we will be picking up?' I dared to ask, as politely as ever. Scar-hand looked at me impatiently.

'You are full of questions, aren't you? I think I have told you enough,' he growled angrily. Without another thought, I threw myself at him and launched a right-hook at his bewildered face. It never connected. Scar-hand merely stepped back one pace, while my fist whizzed past his nose and I lost balance. A sudden blow from the butt of his handgun put me down on all fours and completely disoriented.

'Enough, capitano,' the soothing voice of Scar-hand came through the blinding pain at the back of my head. 'I have dealt with tougher people, so stop making any silly moves.'

I groaned and stood up shakily. Scar-hand stood about five feet away, watching me carefully with his green eyes.

The deck lights had been switched on during this time, and through the bridge front windows, I saw that the crane was being used to launch the last of the three Zodiacs, which seemed to me to be a Classic Mark 2, with a seating capacity of seven persons. I marvelled at the ease with which they had launched and manoeuvred the boats from the heavily rolling deck of our trawler.

After an hour, all three boats returned. Through the rain streaming across the bridge windows, I observed sixteen people coming onboard, carrying several odd-shaped baggage, and finally, a hooded prisoner.

The two henchmen, who had been herding me earlier, joined us on the bridge followed by one of the newcomers. I looked at the new entrant curiously. His bearded face appeared to be familiar. He was dressed like a sheikh complete with a turban and also wore glasses. At a word from Scar-hand, I was immediately taken away at gunpoint and kept standing on the starboard bridge wing in the pouring rain, while he spoke to the sheikh. Just before the bridge wing door closed, I heard the new fellow saying, 'Salaam-ale-kum'.

Then it struck me why his face was so familiar. This was none other than Abu Al-Zohri, a Yemeni national, whose pictures had appeared on television all around the world last year, after Osama Bin Laden had been killed by US Special Forces in Pakistan. This man was one of the top lieutenants of Al-Qaeda. An article in *Time* magazine had stated that the FBI had placed a reward of five million US dollars for any information leading to his capture or death. The hair on the nape of my neck rose and I shivered. It is always easy to imagine how one would deal face-to-face with a terrorist, but in reality, it is a nerve-racking experience. I had not exactly been face-to-face with him, though. I struggled to understand why Al-Zohri would be involved in human-trafficking. No, this was more than that definitely. Looking down at the forward deck, I saw that the newly arrived men had taken shelter in the forecastle store. I wondered who their prisoner was.

The bridge wing door opened, and Scar-hand beckoned me inside. Shivering with cold and wet from head to toe, I went in and looked around. Al-Zohri had left the bridge.

Scar-hand looked at me curiously and then told one of his men to fetch a towel and some dry clothes.

'OK, capitano, time for us to sail for Gibraltar. Prepare for the voyage immediately. Once you have computed the ETA to our new rendezvous point, let one of my men know, and they will call me. Once we get going, one of the new men will take over the steering. Please remember, no heroics. Our passengers are men of extreme violence and even I do not want them to be uncomfortable. By the way, once the new man takes over, get yourself fixed. There is a first-aid kit in the locker under the chart table.'

I nodded, and after drying myself with the towel and changing into ill-fitting clothes that had perhaps never seen soap or water for years, I went to the chart table where a small scale chart of the western Mediterranean had already been placed. I opened a drawer under the chart table to get hold of an eraser and saw several rod magnets. My mind started ticking while contemplating what I could do with them. I grinned and discreetly pocketed them. While I was engrossed in laying out courses and calculating the distances, two men of middle-eastern origins, dressed in jeans and T-shirts, entered the bridge carrying AK-47s pointed at the man they were escorting. He was a short, stout man of middle age, who was clearly the same hooded prisoner whom I had seen earlier. His hands had been handcuffed, and his face appeared to have suffered numerous collisions with fists, boots, and other objects. His right eye was horribly swollen and completely closed. Blood flowing from a cut above his right eyebrow had coagulated around the eye making his appearance even more hideous. My two guards had immediately taken up position near the doorway, as the two middle-eastern men brought their prisoner in front of me. He looked at me through his single good eye, breathing strenuously and grinned, showing off a gaping hole where his two lower front teeth should have been. I was amazed at the man's reaction.

'You the captain?' he asked, with an American accent and grinned again. The two middle-eastern guards looked at me and gestured that this was the new helmsman. They went to the coffee pot and lit up cigarettes, talking quietly, clearly glad to take a break from the harsh weather that they had faced while getting onboard.

'Good God! Who are you then?' I exclaimed in a hushed tone, aware that this might be the only opportunity to exchange information, before somebody who understood English came along and stopped us. The American immediately understood our situation after he had asked me a few whispered questions and concluded that I was not part of any of the gangs on board but just another prisoner like himself.

'Captain, you are in deep trouble. You have to get out as soon as possible.'

'Easier said than done,' I retorted, 'who the hell are you?'

'Take it easy. You can call me Burt. OK, you must understand that this not a simple case of human-trafficking. I work for a specific branch of the CIA. While following up on a lead, I was captured by Al-Qaeda in Yemen, about a month back. They must have planned my capture and led me into a trap because they knew everything about my past.'

'What does your past have to do with anything?' I asked him, puzzled at how his past mattered with my present.

'Look, if you keep interrupting, we may not get time to decide the next move,' he said impatiently and continued, 'I was part of a team working in Guantanamo Bay in 2004 and again in 2010, where we were attempting to, well, let us say, debrief suspected Al-Qaeda members. After our guys took out Bin Laden near Abbotabad, his second-in-command had vowed to take it to the next level. I had unearthed a potential threat to our facility at Guantanamo Bay. Remember the North Korean ship which was detained in Panama in July? That was just a trial run by Al-Qaeda, using the North Koreans to test the feasibility of using the Panama Canal as a conduit for launching a full-scale attack on Guantanamo Bay. The authorities found used fighter aircraft parts and weapons systems, so we could not prove what their main intention was. We have known for a long time that Al-Qaeda was trying to get assistance from the North Koreans, but the arrest of the ship at Panama came as a shock. These guys have now roped in small-time gun runners from Italy to supply them with weapons from old stockpiles in Ukraine. Basically, leftovers from the Cold War era. AK-47s and ammunition are just a tip of the iceberg. These guys have now obtained dirty bombs and missile systems, sufficient to destroy the entire facility at Guantanamo Bay. Problem is that I, and now you, are the only people who know this. In case anything happens to me, you must try and get this information to the nearest US embassy. Is this clear?' he demanded in a fierce whisper, looking alert despite his severe injuries.

It was now clear to me that the terrorists had been interrogating Burt, for a layout and logistics of Guantanamo Bay. This trawler was to be used for staging the attack. It seemed to be an ideal set up. A harmless looking trawler, fishing in the Caribbean Sea would hardly raise suspicions. This was way above any emergency that I had ever encountered at sea. Just then, Scar-hand entered the bridge. He snarled as he saw that I and Burt had been talking and shouted to the two middle-eastern thugs who were busy smoking by the coffee pot. They dropped their cigarettes and jumped to attention. Scar-hand ordered his men to stand guard over us, while he told the other two to guard the entrance door.

'Capitano, I hope for your sake that you have not been wasting time. What have you been talking about?' Scar-hand asked me in a menacing voice. I quickly showed him that the courses had been laid and gave him the ETA to our next rendezvous point, explaining that I was only showing the new helmsman how the steering worked. He relaxed and nodded.

'You, take the wheel. Capitano, tell him the heading to steer,' said Scar-hand and left the bridge. We resumed passage at once. I winked at Burt, who looked at me, puzzled. The bridge was now occupied with self, Burt, Scar-hand's two cronies toting their AK-47s, who had now started taking their duties seriously, and the two middle-eastern terrorists who had planted themselves near the port and starboard bridge wing doors. We took turns at the wheel, I and Burt, changing every two hours, during which time we were strictly monitored by the two Italian thugs, as well as the middle-eastern terrorists. Even the use of the bridge toilet was monitored by one of them. Scar-hand visited the bridge every two hours to check our position which I was plotting on the chart. There was no scope for Burt to exchange any plans with me. The weather had worsened after we had picked up the terrorists, and the visibility was zero. The heavy rain, thick fog, strong wind, and dark gloomy atmosphere was getting on everyone's nerves, as did the severe rolling and pitching of the trawler. At 5 p.m., it was already dark when I took over the steering. I gripped Burt's hand and whispered a few words to him. Burt looked at me as if I was crazy. The alert guard near me immediately yelled and thrust the barrel of his AK-47 into my stomach. I doubled up and collapsed. Burt immediately put his hands up as the second guard aimed his AK-47 at Burt's head, with the safety catch off. I got to my feet and took the wheel as Burt went to get himself some coffee, watched continuously by one of the guards. I hoped Burt had understood my plan. A few minutes later, Scar-hand came to the bridge and peered at the chart to see where I had plotted the trawler's position. I tensed up and swore softly. He looked around, appeared to be satisfied, and left the bridge. At 5.20 p.m, I increased speed to about eighteen knots, and the trawler started pitching and rolling even more heavily. Exactly an hour later, in zero visibility, we ran aground at full speed on the south-east breakwater wall, off Cagliari.

There was an immediate crash of steel and loud grating noise, as the trawler foundered on the concrete and rock structure of the breakwater. I had been holding on tightly to the steering column, but the jarring crash had caught Burt and the four guards unexpectedly. They were thrown across the bridge. Luckily, Burt had fast reflexes and held on to one of the fixed cabinets. The two Italian guards were not so lucky and ended up headlong into the forward bulkhead of the bridge front. The howling wind outside eclipsed the screams and shouts of the people below decks. Burt immediately took stock of the situation and quickly picked up one of the AK-47s. In a fluid movement, he put four short bursts into the chests of the dazed and injured guards. He threw the gun away and picked up the second AK-47, just as the bridge door burst open and Scar-hand leaped in with a gun in his hand. Burt fired at him and got him in the shoulder and chest.

'Quick! Get to the Zodiacs and keep it ready. I am gonna blow up this boat,' shouted Burt. The trawler was now listing heavily to starboard, making it difficult to stand without support.

'You better hurry. She is sinking fast. There is deep water all around here,' I yelled at him. Burt glared at me and ran through the bridge wing door and down the companionway, as I followed him. I had picked up one of the AK-47s lying on the bridge. The terrorists were in a bad shape. Most of them had been seasick and were now pouring out from the damaged forecastle store, in a daze.

Burt fired his AK-47 into their midst until the magazine was empty. We immediately ducked down behind a winch, as retaliatory fire came from some of the terrorists, who had quickly gathered their wits. I felt a searing burning sensation through my left arm, just as I threw him my gun. Looking down, I saw my own blood pouring out from the inner part of my left arm, where a ricocheting bullet had hit me.

'Captain, you are hurt!' yelled Burt, in the roaring wind, and scrambled over to me to inspect the wound.

'It's not too bad. Looks like the bullet went through the soft tissue,' he said as he tore away my shirt and made a tourniquet out of the strips, which he tied around my injury.

'Right, this is the plan. I will draw their fire away from you while you get the Zodiac ready and launched. Wait for me about five metres away, all right?' said Burt calmly. I nodded, realising that my hands were shaking. The next few minutes were extremely disoriented. I can vaguely recollect Burt running down to the fore deck, shooting away at the terrorists and the Italian thugs, while I made my way to the aft deck, where the Zodiacs had been kept lashed under a heavy-duty tarpaulin. I am not sure how I launched the boat, but the next thing I remember was a muffled explosion that knocked me flat in the heaving Zodiac and Burt climbing onboard the boat with a duffel bag. I started the outboard motor, and within thirty minutes, we were thrown by a huge wave on to a rocky shoreline, by my reckoning, somewhere to the south-east of the breakwater. Bruised and battered, I got up and saw Burt sitting twenty feet away holding a hand to his side. I walked over and got a shock when I saw that he had been shot too. He looked up with a grimace and then managed a grin.

'It's not as bad as it looks. The bullet went clean through my side. I missed one of the terrorists. He had been throwing up in the loo,' he chuckled and then gasped as pain shot through his side. I sat down next to him and between us, tried our best to block the exit wound with strips from his shirt. My left arm and hand had become numb with pain, and I could feel my blood throbbing under the tourniquet.

'Where the hell are we, captain?'

'Cagliari in Sardinia,' I said. He looked at me with amazement.

'What the f . . . how . . . how did you manage that?'

'Oh, it was simple really. Before they brought you on the bridge, Scar-hand had told me his plan for the next rendezvous point. That's when I thought of a way to beat him. When I was laying out courses to the second rendezvous point, I found a few spare rod magnets, while looking for an eraser in one of the drawers. If you recall, the trawler only had a magnetic compass. When I had identified Al-Zohri, I knew that this would not be a mere human-trafficking case, but some kind of terrorist activity. So I decided to use the spare magnets to produce an artificial deviation which would go unnoticed by anyone. I decided to produce enough deviation to get an error of about 100°, so when the compass showed a heading of 270, we were actually steering 010°. I had attached those magnets close to the compass bowl with cello-tape, just before you were brought up to the bridge.'

Burt looked at me with deep respect and put out his hand. We grinned at each other and shook hands.

'Brilliant, Captain! I would never have guessed. Should I tell you something? Honestly, I thought it was an accident because of your lousy seamanship. Sorry, I doubted your professional expertise.'

'But I whispered what my intentions were to you during the change of our last watch,' I exclaimed.

Burt looked at me sheepishly and grinned.

'I thought you had lost your wits when you whispered. What I heard was that you wanted ground sardines!' he chuckled, and then we both started laughing. He then asked me the entire story of how I came to be involved in this affair. After I had finished, we discussed what was to be done next. He made me swear that I would not reveal any part of what had happened including me ever having met Burt. If I was asked about my injuries, I was to give them any story other than the truth. He took out two overcoats from his duffel bag and gave one to me.

We shook hands one more time. I saw him walk away into the foggy evening, for the last time. I then walked back to my hotel, which took me over an hour. Thankfully, there were not many people walking around, as the rain was coming down in torrents. A surprised doorman welcomed me back and an even more astonished receptionist handed me the key to my hotel room. After a hot and steaming shower, I cleaned up my various injuries and bandaged the bullet wound, having asked the receptionist for a first aid box, explaining that I had cut myself while shaving. I gave a generous tip to the receptionist from a wad of Euros which I had in my hand luggage. After dressing up, I decided to eat in the restaurant next door. I realised that I had gone without a meal for twenty-four hours. My appetite having been curbed, I went straight back to my room and fell asleep in my clothes.

The next morning, I was to be picked up at 10 a.m., so I got ready, and at 8 a.m., I ordered breakfast from room service and an English newspaper. The weather had improved when I looked out. When my breakfast came, I gobbled up everything and then sat back with a cup of coffee and opened the newspaper. I dropped my cup when I saw the photograph next to the headlines. The headlines read, 'Raid by police on local restaurant'. The photograph was that of Giuseppe Moretti, the late owner of the Ristorante Spensierato, who was found with a bullet hole in his head, said the paper. He had apparently been shot dead without any signs of a fight. A mysterious caller had reported this to the police around 10 p.m. and had also reported that the wine cellar contained an empty wine barrel filled with illegal weapons. The police had immediately raided the place and found the information correct. There was another photograph of a man who was supposed to be the cook working at the restaurant but had gone missing. The police had issued a request to be notified immediately if anyone ever saw this man, who could be identified through a deep scar on his right hand, and was wanted for questioning.

There was also a small article about reports of an explosion heard by some of the residents living near the docks in the late evening. A search of the vicinity had proved fruitless, except for floating debris from what appeared to be wooden crates. Further investigation was to be conducted to find out why the south-east breakwater had been damaged.

I sighed. That's why Moretti had been so glad to see me that evening! And all those questions that he had asked me, now made sense. Burt must have gone and visited Moretti last evening, who had actually been the kingpin. Funny, how everything that I had been involved in for those twenty-four hours had been wiped out of existence. Had the Italian Captain, who worked with Scar-hand, not been injured, none of this would have happened and in all probability, the terrorists would have carried out that attack. As I packed my bags and started towards the elevator, an old proverb came to my mind. It went something like this;

For want of a nail the shoe was lost, for want of a shoe the horse was lost, for want of a horse the rider was lost, for want of a rider the message was lost, for want of a message the battle was lost, and all for the want of a horseshoe nail.

I could not remember the entire proverb, but was sure that for Scar-hand and the terrorists, I had been that nail, albeit, of the wrong size.

9

Death of Hope

'WRITE DOWN EVERYTHING, just as you remember it, sir,' the grey-haired chief of police said sympathetically, as he sat by my bedside in a private ward of the Vancouver General Hospital. 'I will be back tomorrow morning to collect your statement and hand it over to the immigration department for further processing,' he said as he got up, and with a sorrowful shake of his head, went out.

I had been in a daze for the last ten days, in complete depression. I sighed and lay back on bed, my thoughts drifting back to the fateful events of that day on 29 December . . .

'Good evening, ladies and gentlemen. Flight 031 to Prince Rupert is now ready for boarding through gate number B12. All passengers are requested to keep their boarding cards and an identity card ready for a final check at the counter before boarding.'

The announcement over, I found that there were around twenty passengers, including myself, standing in line to board the flight bound from Vancouver BC to Prince Rupert. I was scheduled to join a ship and relieve the Master the next day, on 30 December 2012. The weather that winter had typically caused many frontal depressions, originating from the western part of the Pacific Ocean and ending up in Alaska and north-western Canada. It was minus 5°C outside; while inside the airport, a more sober and habitable temperature of about 18°C was maintained. The winter had brought a lot of snow to this part of the world. I wondered how I was going to acclimatise to this weather when I was on board my ship, standing on the bridge wing during departure from the port.

My flight had already been delayed by three hours due to strong gusting winds accompanied by a flurry of snow. I remembered Prince Rupert, where I had called during summer on another ship. A beautiful jewel of a town, with about 12,000 residents, is connected by Highway 16 to the rest of Canada. Majestic mountains peaked with snowcaps, pleasant weather, and a calm harbour was a memory etched into my mind. To the east of this town lie several ranges of mountains whose slopes are covered with snow all year around.

After duly showing my passport and boarding card, I walked out on to the windy tarmac where the small De Havilland DC8-100 stood forlornly and appeared to be refuelling. I climbed up the short flight of stairs and was directed to my seat by a pretty flight stewardess, whose face appeared to have been frozen into a perpetual smile, either through practice or due to the extreme cold. I located my seat at the tail end of the plane near the left side window. After buckling up my seat belt, I picked up a copy of the in-flight magazine and leafed through the usual articles about great holiday destinations in the north-western part of Canada. The last few pages of the magazine told me how many types of airplanes were operated by this airline. The De Havilland DC8-100 had a seating capacity of thirty-seven passengers, I read and the diagram showed that it had twin-propellers. I peered out of the window into the darkness and could barely make out the three blades of the left-hand propeller in the glow of the light from the open doorway of the plane. The propeller appeared to be lashed down so that it would not start rotating due to the wind. The plane suddenly shook as a gust of wind blew past. All passengers had now boarded, and the door was closed. The stewardess explained the usual safety precautions and emergency exit procedures. She added that we would be experiencing turbulence throughout the flight, so we must always have our seat belts on all the time. Then I must have dozed off, as the next thing I remember is the noise of the propellers as the plane increased speed for taking-off, even as it was being buffeted from side to side by the wind. A tall, bearded, and well-built man of around my age, wearing a red Alpine jacket, blue jeans, and a red balaclava sat on my right, next to the right-hand window.

The plane took off using runway 26R and soon after, executed a turn to starboard to a nor'westerly heading, while continuing its ascent. The turbulence was terrible and alarmed most of the passengers who 'ooohed' and 'aaaahed' at each bump. Levelling off at 10,000 feet, which was the cruising altitude, the captain announced that he was keeping the seat belt sign on and recommended that we remain seated and buckled up at all times. He stated that we would be arriving at Prince Rupert's Digby Airport at 2000 LT. The flight attendant then announced that due to the extreme turbulence, no refreshments would be served until the weather improved. Having seen the weather forecast on TV at the airport earlier, I was sure that she was just saying that to keep us eager and hopeful.

We were more than one hour and twenty minutes into the flight which would have taken us over Texada Island, Seymour Narrows, and Johnstone Straits, and by now, must have been approaching Port Hardy. The pitch-black winter darkness was impenetrable, and I could not see anything from the small window, other than the flashing of our navigation lights through the flurry of falling snow. Suddenly the plane lurched into what seemed to be a vortex and did a free-fall of almost 500 feet. Some of the passengers yelled out in alarm, and I found myself tensed, gripping the armrests of my seat. The pilot must have been an ace, as he manoeuvred the plane carefully out of the low pressure pocket. The plane steadied for a minute. And then all hell broke loose.

A loud bang came from the right-hand side of the aircraft, which was instantaneously followed by a ripping sound, as one of the starboard propeller fins broke off, pierced the hull of the aircraft, tore through the two men sitting in seats 4G and 4H, and cut into the overhead luggage compartment on the opposite side, embedding itself somewhere deep inside. There was complete chaos as the aircraft plunged downwards and to starboard. The screams of the passengers were muted due to the whooshing sub-zero wind which entered the hole that had been made by the propeller fin and caused the cabin temperature to plummet rapidly. It was too difficult to breathe, as the frigid rushing air numbed my lungs. The pilots struggled with the distressed aircraft, trying to keep as much control as they could. The plane appeared to be fighting with itself, as if trying to shake off its passengers, as it shook from side to side and up and down violently, unable to withstand the fury of the winds, snow, and the effect of the damaged starboard propeller.

'Mayday, mayday, mayday. This is Flight 031, 031, 031, mayday. I have a damaged starboard propeller . . . losing altitude rapidly . . . my position is 5126N 12607W, over,' yelled the pilot frantically into the microphone. He must have switched on the passenger address system by mistake since the message came through the speakers overhead.

'Flight 031, this is Digby Control, roger. We will alert emergency services, BCSARA and NSR immediately. Can you make it to Digby airport? Over.'

'Digby Control, 031, negative. I have lost most of the controls. Over.'

'Flight 031, Digby Control. Hang in there!'

British Columbia Search and Rescue Association (BCSARA) and North Shore Rescue (NSR) Team Society were the two dedicated organisations which carried out SAR operations in this region. While the BCSARA was divided into twelve rescue zones and had a large amount of resources, the NSR was a team of forty highly skilled volunteers based out of North Vancouver.

The plane was losing altitude rapidly while gyrating in wide circles and banked heavily to the right. The pilots were dazed at first, but their training kicked in and they fought the aircraft, trying, almost willing the plane to come back to an even keel. Miraculously, a strong updraft of wind from the starboard side caused the plane to become upright. However, the pilots were unable to control the heading, which was now due east, being pushed onwards by an 80-knot tail wind. Shouts of sheer terror and screams continued as we were rocked unceremoniously in our seats like rag dolls. The plane flew on for about thirty minutes in almost a straight easterly heading before again banking to the right and dropping rapidly.

The last thing that I remembered was a loud, bone-jarring crash and a detached feeling as I saw with unbelieving, tear-filled eyes that the front of the aircraft was moving away from me, as darkness enveloped all around and I momentarily lost consciousness. The tail section of the plane had hit a mountain ledge, broken off from the rest of the aircraft, and miraculously been thrown on the eastern side of the mountain on which was a steep slope, covered with snow. The middle and forward section of the aircraft disappeared into the dark void of the night and the falling snow. The aft section of the aircraft slid down the slope, gathering speed, with the tail pointed forward, and after about five crazy minutes, hit a rocky outcropping and came to a sudden halt.

When I opened my eyes, the first thing that hit me was the complete silence and darkness. I was still strapped in my seat and could barely make out the silhouette of the passenger sitting on my right. He seemed to be extremely still. The shock of what I had just experienced gradually seeped into my woozy mind. I had been through an air crash and survived! My hands started shaking involuntarily, as the adrenalin kicked in. It was terribly cold, and it had even penetrated the four layers of clothing that I was wearing. I slowly tried moving my limbs and neck to ascertain that nothing was broken. There did not appear to be any broken bones in my hands or legs, but my neck hurt terribly, and I had a huge bump on my forehead, which was probably caused when I had hit my head on the seat in front. Thankfully, I felt no signs of external bleeding. Removing my seat belt, I stood up cautiously and banged my head on the overhead locker, which must have opened when we crashed. I remembered that I had a small flashlight in my carry-on bag, which I immediately retrieved. I took out my cell phone and switched it on. I waited for a few minutes, but there was no signal. Switching on the flashlight, I pointed it at my co-passenger and moved over to help him.

'Hey! Wake up!' I said as I tried to push him to an upright position. He groaned, and his eyes flickered. He was bleeding from his forehead. I looked around and spotted a blanket which I used to wipe off the blood and then tied it up around his injury to stop the bleeding. Five minutes later, he was reasonably back to full consciousness.

'Wha . . . what happened?' he asked in a weak voice.

'We crashed. Try moving your legs and hands.'

He did as told and except for an injured knee, he appeared to be fine.

'What's your name?' I asked.

'Kevin. What's yours?' I told him.

'Looks like, we are the only survivors.'

'Jesus Christ!'

'Look, we have to try and call for assistance. Do you have a cell phone? I can't get a signal on mine.'

He groped around and switched on his mobile phone. We waited for a few minutes but with a similar result.

'Where the hell are we?' asked Kevin, the fear apparent in his voice. I flashed the torch outside. We both gasped in surprise. We were inside some kind of a cave. Scrambling out of the tail section, we got down and surveyed our surroundings. The telltale signs where the tail end had slid were clearly visible on the ground. We followed the scrapped markings for about fifty feet over a steep incline, when we came to what appeared to be the mouth of a narrow crevasse overlooking an ice cliff. The wind outside was howling like a banshee. After a quick look around, we came back to what was left of our plane. There was no way we could go outside. We would be dead within minutes in that wind chill. Kevin went to his backpack and removed a flashlight.

'I think we might get a mobile signal if we stand close to the entrance,' he said. We took out our mobile phones and made our way back near the entrance. After several futile minutes, we gave up. I suddenly remembered that my mobile phone had a GPS function. I switched it on and waited for the satellites to be acquired. About five minutes later, I got the coordinates, while Kevin looked on at what I was doing.

'OK, at least we have our coordinates. I will try and figure out where we are exactly,' I said. Returning to the aircraft, I got my laptop out and waited for it to start up, thankful that I had a fully charged battery. I opened an e-maps program that I always carried with me on ships and then fed in the coordinates. The computer took a few seconds and then zeroed in on our location. I zoomed in and saw what was marked on my e-chart as Mount Waddington.

'We are on the east face of Mount Waddington,' I said to him, reading off the notations on the e-chart. It showed the height of the mountain as 4019 metres (13,186 feet).

'Shit! That's awful! Are you sure?' he exclaimed, now appearing nervous.

I looked at him curiously.

'Well, as best as I can figure out. Is it a well-known place?'

'Mate, Mount Waddington is the tallest mountain in BC. This range of mountains is completely uninhabited. There are people who come here for hiking and trekking, but that's in summer. We are totally screwed, man. Also, this is grizzly bear country.'

I digested this piece of information silently. Our chances of survival were poor. Even if we managed to survive the cold, we would not survive without food or water. I recalled what I had seen on a documentary on Discovery Channel about bears. They would sleep off the entire winter in a trance-like state known as hibernation. I had wondered if humans would be able to do that too. Now, I just hoped that none of the bears suffered from insomnia.

'Do you think anyone will come looking for us in this weather?' I queried. Kevin thought for a while.

'Doubt it, mate. The BCSARA and the NSR are well equipped and trained for mountain rescue work, but I don't think anyone would dare to come out now.'

Thinking over our situation, we decided that the best way was to go and explore the cavern within which we had fallen. Going out through the entrance of the cave and into the cold howling blizzard outside was definitely out of question, as we would have frozen to death within minutes. We rummaged through what was left of the aircraft for any useful items. Our search was fruitful when we checked some of the baggages in the overhead locker. A few tins of salmon and corned beef, two bottles of water, a bottle of aspirin, six bars of chocolates, four flashlights, and a few clothes were what we found. I wondered whether the people in the front of the aircraft had survived. Perhaps they were also lying somewhere out there, half-buried in the snow? I checked the strong emotion which was urging me to go outside and search for them. It would have been absolutely futile in the present circumstances.

We filled up our backpacks with whatever we could carry and started walking into the guts of the cave, which was filled to the brim with darkness. The sloping cave floor was at an angle of about 30°, so we could easily manage to walk down the rocky slope without much hindrance, other than that from a few boulders sitting in our way. After an hour of this, we reached a point where the chamber diverged into two. We decided to take the left one first and see where it took us. The left passage was about five feet wide and about ten feet high. Kevin led the way and I followed. The air was surprisingly breathable but dry and terribly cold. After four hours, we took a break and settled down to eat a meal. We quickly dozed off after the meal.

When we woke up, it was 10 a.m. of the next day. 'I would have been boarding my ship now,' I thought. Sleeping in that frigid cave had caused my joints to ache, and my bruises had become extremely painful. I saw that Kevin was suffering likewise, so we gulped down two aspirins each. We finished packing up, and after a hasty toilet, resumed our march into the gloom. This time, I led the way. We had decided to conserve our flashlights, so only the lead man would carry a torch. After six hours of trekking, we were exhausted and sat down for a bit and took a gulp of water. We had to ration our water too, as there had been no sign of an underground stream or rivulet. After resting for an hour, we started again. The interior of the rock tunnel was undulating, so we never knew whether we were above or below our point of origin. We must have travelled about thirty kilometres that day, by the time we stopped for the night. We rarely spoke to each other, as we tried to conserve our energy. As we ate that night, I was suddenly aware that this may have been a very foolish method of trying to escape. We would have been better off waiting at the mouth of the cave until the weather had cleared. When I voiced my feelings to Kevin, he acknowledged that he felt the same way. Then and there we decided to head back the same way that we had come, until we reached the tail section of our plane. With this happy thought, I fell asleep.

The next morning, 31 December, we headed back. I could not resist making a rock engraving with my name on the cave surface, as if to leave a message to anyone who might one day come here. Kevin did the same when he observed what I was doing. We had to cover about forty-five kilometres ahead of us to reach our origin. Unfortunately, we had finished all our water. It was 2.35 p.m. when Kevin who was leading the way suddenly exclaimed and stopped, causing me to bump into him. Looking ahead, I saw what had made him halt. It was a complete puzzle. There were four pathways leading into four different caverns ahead of us. There was no way to be completely sure, from which entrance we had come.

'Geez! No wonder it is called the Mystery Mountain! So what do we do now, captain?' asked Kevin. I felt irritated for no reason.

'Let's take the one on the extreme left,' I suggested after a pause.

We went through the left corridor and must have walked three kilometres, when we entered a cavern. The ground had now become uneven, and the air in the cavern was even colder. Although there was no wind, I was sure the temperature was well below minus 25°C. It was as if we had entered an empty deep freezer of the Abominable Snowman. After twenty more minutes of walking, Kevin stopped once again and shushed me. In the silence, we could hear rushing water.

'Must be an underground river' I said. 'Let's take a look.'

About two hours later, we came to a narrow ledge from where I saw water spraying out with high pressure from a huge fissure in the rock wall on our left. The temperature here was even colder than before. Taking out his water bottle, Kevin went forward to the edge of the precipice, keeping the flashlight aimed at the torrential stream, barely four feet below where we stood. Just as he bent down to fill up his bottle, he slipped on the moss-covered rocks and with a scream of terror, plunged into the turbulent water. I shouted in frustration as I had no chance to even try and assist him. One moment he was right there in front of me, and the next, he was gone. The sudden darkness had blinded me, since Kevin had our last torch. Like a blind man trying to find his way, I searched around with my hands and sat down on the rocks, shivering with cold. My back was sore from carrying the heavy backpack for so long, so I removed it and let it fall on the rocky ledge beside me. Crawling on my hands and legs, I slithered towards the place where Kevin had slipped. Looking down, I saw the loom of a light, just below the surface of the rushing water about ten feet away to my right. It was the flashlight! Maybe Kevin was close by and hurt. The drop from the ledge was barely four feet, so I tried to get a foothold and move towards the flashlight. Fifteen agonising minutes later, I was close to the flashlight and stretched out my hand to grab it. That's when my feet slipped and I fell into the rushing torrent.

*   *   *

My eyes flickered open. I was lying on my back, covered with blankets. I realised that I was extremely cold and shivering horribly. The next moment, two persons with masks on their faces peered down at me. One of them said something to me while the other held up a steel tube. I passed out as something hissed under my left ear.

When I regained consciousness, I slowly moved my eyes to see my surroundings. I was not cold anymore, but there was a throbbing pain in my head.

'Hello. So you have finally woken up, have you?' said a soft, female voice from somewhere behind my head. I was still lying on my back under several blankets. With an effort, I tried to sit up but groaned in pain and fell back on my pillow. I looked up as the woman came around and peered down at me. She had a mask on her face and a doctor's cap on her head, but I saw that she had pretty blue eyes.

'Take it easy. You shouldn't try to get up yet. I am Dr Delaney. What's your name?' she asked. I assumed that she was smiling behind the mask, the way the corners of her eyes crinkled.

So I was in a hospital. How the hell did I get here? The last thing I remembered was falling into the torrential underground river.

'Where am I?' I croaked. The sound of my voice felt strange and hollow. My throat was completely dry.

'You are at Vancouver General Hospital. What's your name?' she asked again and peered into my eyes with a small torch.

'Captain Jay Gordon,' I whispered raspingly, not sure what she would do with it. She probably needed it for the hospital bill.

'Well, captain, everything looks normal. Now, you just lie back and relax while I call the senior doctor to take a look at you, OK?' she said in a soothing voice.

I did as told and wondered how I had ended up in the hospital. Between the time of my fall and the present was a gap which I felt needed an explanation. I moved my neck and looked at my surroundings. It was a well-equipped hospital room with some curious-looking gadgets all around. I had been to hospitals several times but had never seen equipment like this before. A few minutes later, the door opened, and Dr Blue Eyes came in with another doctor, as promised.

'Hello there, young man! You really can sleep, can't you? You have been asleep for almost two weeks now. By the way, I am Dr Schneider,' said the new doctor, in a merry voice. He looked to be about sixty.

'Hello, doctor,' I said and extended my right hand towards him from under my blankets. I realised that several tubes and sensors were connected to the back of my hand. Dr Schneider took my hand delicately, so as not to disturb the position of all those sensors and tubes. He peered into my eyes exactly as Dr Blue Eyes had done and nodded in satisfaction.

'Great! You seem to have recovered almost completely. Do you have any pain?' asked Dr Schneider.

'A dull throbbing in my head, doctor,' I said.

'That will soon go away when you have had some solid food. We have been feeding you intravenously since you were brought here,' he explained.

'Where . . . where did you find me, doctor?'

'Well, I didn't find you. It was the police who brought you here. What were you thinking, swimming in Horseshoe Bay in winter time?' he cackled at his own joke.

'Horseshoe Bay?'

'That's right. The police found you literally half-frozen in a block of ice, about a mile from the marina. Thanks to a local fisherman who spotted a semi-naked body floating near his favourite fishing spot and immediately called the police. Here, drink this,' said Dr Schneider as he offered me a glass with a murky-looking fluid. Dr Blue Eyes helped me up into a sitting position by pressing a button near my hand, which inclined the bed from my waist up. I took the glass and gulped it down.

'Are you feeling good enough to answer some questions?' asked Dr Schneider seriously. I nodded.

'Right. There is a police inspector who has been waiting to interview you. Dr Delaney, will you locate him and tell him that our patient has returned from dreamland? Thank you,' said Dr Schneider.

A few minutes later, Dr Delaney returned with the cop. He was a typical-looking cop with short cropped hair and straight backed.

'How are you feeling, sir?' queried the inspector with a smile.

'Good enough, inspector,' I replied.

'I know you have had a bad time, but I need to get some information from you, OK? Let's start with your name, age, address, next of kin and their contact number, your occupation, and the name of the company that you work for,' said the inspector, taking out a legal pad and pen. I gave him the required information which he jotted down quietly.

'What date is it, inspector?'

'It's 16 January, captain,' he replied. Dr Blue Eyes was observing us from her corner seat near Dr Schneider.

I felt anxiety overwhelming me. I was to have joined my ship, at Prince Rupert on 30 December, eighteen days ago. I was sure that my family back home and the managers from my company in Hong Kong may be thinking that I had died in the air crash. I leaned up forward on one elbow and looked intently at the cop.

'Inspector, there must be people wondering about me. You must inform the airport authorities immediately that I am alive and well. My family must be thinking I am dead!' I said anxiously, words tumbling over one another in their haste to come out of my mouth.

'Take it easy, sir. Why do you want us to inform the airport authority? Are you a pilot?' asked the inspector, puzzled at my outburst. Dr Schneider stood up and went to check one of the monitors behind my head.

'No, I am a mariner, inspector. I was flying from Vancouver to Prince Rupert on the flight which crashed somewhere near Mount Waddington on 29 December. Haven't you even heard about it? Flight 031. There were about twenty passengers on board,' I asked him, looking at his confused expression.

I was alarmed. The inspector's reaction made no sense at all. I was sure that the moment they heard my name, there would be a scramble to inform the right authorities that they had found at least one survivor from the crash. As I knew it, airlines immediately printed out a passenger manifest if one of their planes was ever lost and distributed it to law enforcement agencies.

The inspector looked at Dr Schneider with a query in his eyes. But he was standing behind me, so I could not see what gestures he might have made. The inspector nodded and rose from his seat.

'I will see you later, sir. Get some rest for now,' he said, and nodding to Dr Delaney, he went out.

'Look, doctor. Just, what the hell is going on?' I burst out, while trying to turn around to face him.

'Take it easy. It appears that you may have a concussion. I will give you something to relax and you just lie down and rest, OK?' said Dr Schneider, as Dr Delaney quickly went to a cabinet and prepared a strange-looking metallic pipe with green and red lights on it. I was not sure if what the doctor had just said was true. I was feeling light-headed and everything seemed to be unreal around me, the crash, the journey under the mountains, the slip into the underground river, and finally this. I felt cold steel on my neck, which was immediately followed by a hiss. I started feeling woozy and felt the bed reclining as I passed out.

When I woke up, Dr Schneider was sitting near a work desk in the corner. There were two more men with him, whom I presumed to be doctors, looking at their attire.

'Good morning, Dr Schneider,' I said from my bed. The three men jumped up as if they had been caught out at peek-a-boo.

'Well, well, well. And how are we feeling today?' said the good doctor jovially and came around to my bedside.

'I am feeling perfectly fine. Is there any news from my family?' I asked eagerly. He looked at me for a while and shook his head.

'We are waiting for the police to locate your family and get back to us,' he said.

'Doctor, at least let me call my home or my company office in Hong Kong so that they know that I am all right!' I said hotly. The doctor looked at me calmly.

'Wait a moment please,' he said and walked out of the room. The two other doctors followed him out.

I had had enough of this nonsense. It was almost as if I was being kept a prisoner. Deciding that enough was enough, I got up from bed and ripped off all the tubes and sensors connected to my body. There was a hospital gown hanging on one of the pegs behind the door, which I quickly slipped into. My legs felt a weak, as if the muscles had lost their strength. It was almost as if I had not used them for a long time. Flexing, my arms felt the same way. I hobbled out of the doorway and ran into the inspector who was just about to enter my room with another cop.

'Here! Where do you think you are off to?' he exclaimed, holding my arm in a tight grip and leading me back inside. I had no strength to fight him off, so I sat down on my bed, just as Dr Schneider and his two colleagues came running.

'Listen, you guys. At least tell me what the hell is happening? Why are you being so secretive?' I demanded feebly. The two doctors pushed me back on the bed but let the tubes and sensors remain hanging.

'The inspector and the superintendent here have just brought some news,' said Dr Schneider. The superintendent pulled up a chair near me and introduced himself while the others remained standing.

'Now, sir, I want you to think clearly and tell me everything that you can remember. You told the inspector yesterday that you were a survivor from a plane crash, is that correct?'

I nodded.

'Fair enough. If you give me all the information that you can, I will be able to help you, you understand? So let's begin,' said the superintendent in a calm and reasonable voice. He switched on a small gadget which must have been a voice recorder.

I told them the whole story, beginning from the time I was at Vancouver airport until the time I found myself in the hospital, not leaving a single bit out. When I had finished, I could see the incredulous look on their faces. I asked for a glass of water which Dr Schneider immediately provided.

'OK. Now, I want you to hear me out calmly,' said the superintendent, coolly observing me. 'Based on the information that you gave to the inspector yesterday, we have checked up with the airport authorities at Vancouver as well as Prince Rupert. Firstly, there is no record of any flight called 031, taking off or crashing on 29 December. Secondly, the company that you stated you work for does not exist. Thirdly, we tried to contact the number you had given for your next of kin. The number does not exist. The home address that you provided, well, it is incorrect as there is a different house in its location. And lastly, we find no immigration records of you having entered Canada at all! Is there anything else that you can tell us so that we can sort this out, or will you admit that it was just a cock-and-bull story that you have been feeding us? You might as well admit that you were attempting suicide by jumping into frozen waters or that you are a bloody refugee!'

I was completely numb with this shocking information. What the hell could have happened to the world in three weeks? My mind whirled in confusion as I thought about something that would assist the cops. Then it struck me.

'What about the actual site of the air crash? Has anyone checked the area for debris or wreckage?' I demanded, excitedly.

'Like I explained, there is no record of any aircraft being lost in BC,' the superintendent said impatiently.

'But if there is evidence of the wreckage on Mount Waddington, would that not substantiate what I have been telling you?' I demanded in anger. 'Why were these cops not looking for proof of my story?' I wondered.

The superintendent sighed in exasperation.

'And where on the mountain would you like us to search? It is a huge area to cover!'

'I remember the coordinates very clearly,' I said and gave them to him, which was jotted down by the inspector. The superintendent got up, the interview clearly over.

'We will make inquiries and get back to you. Meanwhile, you must stay in this hospital until further notice,' he said glaring at me. Clearly, he suspected that I was pulling their legs. The cops left soon after, and I was left alone with Dr Schneider and his two colleagues, whom I noticed had been taking notes during the interview.

'These two colleagues of mine are from the psychiatric department and are helping us in determining your case,' said Dr Schneider, by way of introduction. The two men pulled their chairs near my bed and questioned me over four hours, until I was completely exhausted. Finally, around 7 p.m., they left.

I spent the next six days in the hospital, during which time Dr Delaney told me that the psychiatrists had found nothing unusually wrong with me. Due to my weak condition, I slept most of the time, assisted by the drugs, with which the doctors were injecting me. My bruises were healing very well, though I still had difficulty using my feet and hands as the muscles were still getting back into shape with the help of a physiotherapist who visited me daily. On 23 January, the cops came back followed closely by Dr Schneider and Dr Delaney. This time I was sitting up in my bed with a mug of coffee in my hand.

'Any luck, sir?' I queried eagerly, as he sat down in front of me.

The superintendent looked at me but remained silent, as he gathered his thoughts.

'The wreckage of the tail section of an aircraft has been found, exactly as you said,' he said quietly. Dr Schneider and Dr Delaney looked up in surprise. I was thrilled and grinned in delight.

'So now you know that I was not making it all up!' I exclaimed, much to the discomfort of the superintendent and the inspector, while I rejoiced that at least now they could get things straightened out.

'I don't really know how to put this,' said the superintendent, scratching his chin. I had not seen him or the inspector so nervous earlier. I wondered where he was leading this conversation. All he had to do was find out the remaining details from the airlines and let me contact my family back home.

The superintendent hesitatingly said, 'You see, we did confirm from the airport about the crash.'

Dr Schneider and Dr Delaney leaned forward in anticipation while the inspector remained standing in the corner, fidgeting with his hands nervously. The superintendent took out a several sheets of paper from a file he was carrying.

'This is an extract from the findings of the Air Transport Safety Board dated 31 January 2013, which I am reading out to you,' he said. I and the two doctors looked at him as if he had gone crazy.

'A preliminary investigation into the loss of Flight 031 by the ATSB found clear evidence of metal fatigue in blade number three of the starboard propeller. The penetration of the broken blade into the hull frame of the aircraft caused a short circuit in the main avionics and electronic controls. These were the primary causes for the aircraft to lose directional and altitude control. When Digby Tower received a distress alert from the pilot at 1925 LT, they immediately alerted Vancouver airport who in turn issued an emergency alert to rescue services, Coast Guard, and the RCMP. Digby Tower had been tracking the aircraft on radar since 1907 LT, but lost radar contact when the aircraft went into a blind sector north-east of Mount Waddington at 1945 LT. On 2 January the weather improved and all efforts were made by rescue helicopters from the Coast Guard, private boat owners, and mountain rescue units from NSR and BCSAR to locate the stricken aircraft. They suspended the search at 0130 LT on 4 January, when the weather started deteriorating. It was ascertained that Flight 031 did crash on Mount Waddington on 29 December 2012. The wreckage from the front section of the aircraft was located by a team comprising of BCSARA, NSR, and Coast Guard personnel in the area south-east of the peak, scattered over two kilometres on 3 January at 1437 LT. There were no survivors. However, they could not locate the broken tail section of the aircraft. Until now,' said the superintendent and gulped down a glass of water. We were all leaning forward expectantly. He gave us all an uneasy look and continued.

'That is the end of the extract which I have with me from that report. However, the latest information after locating the tail section is like this. As per the coordinates that you gave us last week, the BCSARA found the tail section inside a cave that could be accessed only through a crevasse which is inaccessible by foot. They had to lower the rescue teams by helicopter. The lead team reported that they found the frozen body of one person, in one of the tunnels that they explored in the cavern. From the autopsy, he appeared to have died from drowning. The body was in a perfectly preserved condition due to the permafrost.'

He paused again and his face took on a blanched look. He looked up at us as we waited with our breaths held.

'The airline records confirmed that as per the passenger manifest and photographs, the body was that of Kevin Baldwin who was seated in the last row on the right,' said the superintendent, in a whisper.

We sat in stunned silence. My mind was in turmoil. Poor Kevin! Although we had met only for a short time, we had become good friends.

The superintendent looked at me with something bordering fear. He cleared his throat again and said, 'The passenger manifest also names Jay Gordon, who was seated in this row on the left.'

Dr Schneider and Dr Delaney gasped in horror. I looked at them quizzically. 'What the hell were they so terrified of?' I wondered.

The superintendent looked at me with terror reflecting in his eyes, and continued, 'Captain, you were found in Horseshoe Bay, floating in the water, almost completely trapped in a block of ice. As you know, the aircraft crashed on 29 December 2012. What you do not know is . . . is . . . that . . . today is 23 January 2113. The crash occurred 100 years back. You . . . you should have been long dead!'

10

Just Not Cricket

THE EFFRONTERY WITH which Anthony Wells, the opening batsman of the English cricket team, hammered the opposition bowlers over the ropes with ease and regularity was becoming legendary. In his career so far, he had scored seventeen centuries in twenty-one, one-day matches. This had caused immense excitement and speculation in the cricketing world. Pundits all over had already started placing his name in the same column as legendary greats like Don Bradman, Brian Lara, and Sachin Tendulkar. Statisticians argued incessantly over the future of this new wizard of cricket, as they tried to project the zenith of his batting curve. Newspapers and tabloids of all cricket-playing nations published extensive articles on his batting skills, before and after each match, wherever he was playing.

It was just after the final of the Tri-Nation series at Lords, which was played between England and Pakistan, the West Indies having been knocked out of contention, when all hell broke loose. England, in spite of being the weaker side, won the closely contested final by two runs, in which Anthony Wells had scored a shaky 104 before he was caught at mid-off. A bookie by the name of Sam was apprehended by the London Metropolitan Police, after they received a tip-off through an anonymous phone call that a few of the players from one of the teams in the final match had been involved in match-fixing. Sam was picked up from a tiny bed and breakfast in east London, from where he had been operating, along with his laptop and several cell phones. The media went berserk with this latest scandal and tried to outdo each other in reporting breaking news. During the interrogation, when Sam finally broke down and started exposing it all, the Met handed over their findings to the Crown Prosecution Service, and the matter went to the Crown Court, after it had passed the evidential stage as well as the public interest stage. The Magistrates' Court was completely bypassed, as this was considered to be a high-profile case. Players from both the teams were put on a 'no-fly' roster and firmly informed that they were not allowed to leave London until further notice. When four players from the Pakistani team were arrested on the basis of Sam's evidence, and led away by the police, the Pakistani team managers immediately protested in every way possible, even calling for a press conference during which they vehemently denied any wrongdoing. The Pakistani government also entered the fray by sending a formal letter of protest to the British embassy in Islamabad.

The four Pakistani players were produced before the Crown court, and the case prolonged for a week during which a considerable amount of evidence was gathered and produced which confirmed that Sam was not lying. Due to the high-profile nature of the case, the commissioner of the

Metropolitan Police briefed a group of cabinet ministers who were assigned to study the matter. He confirmed that yet another scandalous affair had reared its ugly head. The reputation of the Pakistani team had already suffered a serious blow in 2010, during a similar match-fixing scandal. The cabinet ministers screamed for blood, determined to punish the guilty. The prime minister decided that the public should be given all the information and directed the commissioner to address a press conference, supported by two of the stalwarts of English cricket, Lord Percival and Lord Theodore. The two Lordships were one of the few aristocrats who had an impeccable record of fair play.

The very same evening, a press conference was arranged. The podium was shared by the commissioner with Lord Percival and Lord Theodore, the two highly respected gentlemen, each of whom were patrons of two different County Cricket teams. The televised press conference was attended by journalists from all major newspapers. The briefing was opened by the commissioner, in which he read out a statement.

'Ladies and gentlemen, could I have your attention, please? I will be reading out a statement and will not be taking any questions,' he said, as the crowd became silent.

'A week ago, the Metropolitan Police received a tip-off that the final match between England and Pakistan had been subject to a spot-fixing deal between a bookie named Sam and four Pakistani players. After carrying out an initial investigation, the Metropolitan Police confirmed that there was credence to this accusation. The four Pakistani players accused of match-fixing were produced before the Crown, and after a week long court battle, we are certain to get a full conviction. The evidence given by the bookie called Sam, of large cash payments having been made to the four players, was found in four of the lockers at Victoria Station. Keys to these lockers were found in the players' hotel rooms, concealed within their clothes. The bookie, Sam, approached the four players separately, two days before the final, and assured them a payment of 20,000 pounds each, to score less than ten runs in any five overs that they batted in. The four players are Rana, Mehboob, Riazuddin, and Saleh. These four and the bookie will continue to remain in our custody in separate cells until tomorrow, pending the verdict from the court. Thank you for your attention.'

As the commissioner and his two companions rose, the air became thick with questions from all the journalists gathered there, which they directed at the backs of the three departing men. The journalists immediately ran at top speed to their individual offices to file their reports and amazingly, even passed by a few pubs on their way, without stopping for a spot.

Later that evening, a curious incident took place. The police received another anonymous call, in which the name of another bookie, Trent, surfaced. Trent was picked up from the cross-channel ferry terminal at Dover, just as he was about to flee to Europe. During the subsequent investigation, Trent sang the song favoured by the police. This time around, they were not so sure that they liked the tune. An uneasy interrogator went up to the chief inspector and told him what he had learnt from Trent. The chief inspector was flabbergasted by the revelation, swore loudly, and went to the commissioner with this news. The bewildered commissioner called his best team of investigators and had a closed-door conference on how they had to proceed.

That night, the commissioner of the Metropolitan Police briefed the same group of cabinet ministers and the PM on this new development, which baffled them completely. The PM dismissed the commissioner and told him to wait for his call for further instructions. After discussion with the Cabinet, the PM called the commissioner and told him to present the facts as they were, during the next day in court.

The new evidence was also submitted before the Crown court on the following day, and the case prolonged further, for another week. The four dejected Pakistani players were surprised when they were driven to the court to find more charges framed against them. Right from the start, all four had denied the accusations. During the trial, at which the media was not allowed, the facts of the new development were presented. The right honourable Judge first heard the plea of the defence counsel who demanded to know that on basis of these new facts, how could the accused be held responsible for match-fixing? He said it was inexplicable that the bookie called Trent had allegedly paid a substantial amount to the four Pakistani players to ensure that they scored at least six runs in each over for five consecutive overs, while the bookie named Sam had paid them a similar amount to score less than ten runs in those same five overs. The defence counsel argued that the match-fixing efforts of either of the bookies appeared to have been unsuccessful as none of his four clients had done what was allegedly required of them.

The recording of the final match was produced as evidence and was played for all those present in the courtroom. The video-graphic evidence clearly showed that in the five overs during which the opening pair of Rana and Mehboob batted, they had scored twenty runs, while the partnership of Riazuddin and Omar, coming in at one down and two down, had produced twenty-two runs in five overs. The defence counsel rested their case.

The prosecution counsel stated that even if the four players had not carried out what was required of them by the bookies, the facts of the case clearly showed that an attempt had been made by the same four players to gain monetary benefits from the match, to which the defence counsel immediately objected stating that his clients had not gained anything out of the so-called match-fixing. He went on to state that the mere presence of a set of keys fitting the lockers at Victoria Station or the lockers at Heathrow, which were found in the hotel rooms of his clients, could not be construed as 'clear grounds' for accusing them of match-fixing. The prosecution then stated that it was clear that each of the keys found with the players opened a separate locker at Victoria Station, where the players would be headed before going to Heathrow airport. The prosecution stated that as per the investigation report from the police, they had found 20,000 pounds in cash in each of the lockers. A search of the lockers at Heathrow airport had also unearthed 20,000 pounds in each of the lockers, and thus, it was clear that the four accused were hoping to gather the cash from the two separate lockers allotted to each of them, which made eight lockers in all, before boarding their flight back to Karachi.

The judge heard arguments from both sides with equal gravity. Towards evening of that Friday, he decided that he would issue the final verdict on the following Monday, after the weekend. The four Pakistani players and the two bookies were sent back into the custody of the London Metropolitan Police, for the weekend. During the weekend, one of the tabloids, whose journalists were experts in the art of scooping up dirt, managed to get hold of a three-week-old photograph of two of the four accused Pakistani players, sitting in a fashionable nightclub along with Sam, which led to wide-spread uproar in the cricketing world. The Pakistani High Commission accused the tabloid of digitally morphing the photographs, which later proved to be true.

On Monday, the judge delivered the verdict. This time around, journalists were allowed into the courtroom. The judge simplified the statement, the gist of which was that while there were indications that the four accused Pakistani players were somehow involved in the scandal, the evidence was merely circumstantial and hence inconclusive. He asked the Metropolitan Police if they could provide more evidence to give credibility to the case for prosecution, to which the commissioner shook his head. The judge then dismissed the case and exonerated the four accused Pakistani players. He, however, warned the representatives of the ICC and the Pakistan Cricket Board (PCB) that they should keep an eye on the four Pakistani players in the future and should take appropriate action to avoid tarnishing the image of this gentleman's game. The judge then directed the police to remand the two bookies for one month and carry out a full investigation into the match-fixing deal. The judge stated that the only fact which could be proved was that unknown persons had been involved in trying to get the match fixed, due to the cash found in the lockers and the evidence of the two bookies. The men and women of the press were largely disappointed and headed to the nearest pub, before heading back to file their reports.

Late one evening, three days after the case of the match-fixing scandal had been concluded, a black Bentley Continental glided noiselessly in the light drizzle on Brompton Road. On reaching the corner, the Bentley slowed down, turned left on Egerton Terrace, and then took a right turn on Egerton Crescent. It slowed down further and stopped in front of one of the homes. Egerton Crescent was the most expensive street to live on, in the entire country, and catered only to the elite. The door in front of which the Bentley had come to a halt was one of the several neatly aligned homes of the super-rich. This one was actually owned collectively by a group of aristocrats, who had converted it into a hyper-exclusive club. Lord Percival got down from the Bentley, carrying a brown brief case, and headed for the door, after a brief glance all around. He took out a white key card from his pocket, which had no logos or markings, and inserted it into a slot on the door. Each member had a similar key card, which made their entry into the club unobtrusive. A smartly dressed butler welcomed

Lord Percy and took his hat and coat. The interior of the club was richly adorned. The thick carpet would have been an impediment to walk through, had it been even a few millimetres thicker. Several seats were occupied by other members of this elite club. The seating arrangement was aligned in such a way that the occupants of each table could discreetly conduct their business, without anyone eavesdropping on them. Lord Percy entered the room and looked around, nodding to a few of the inmates, and then proceeded towards a far corner where Lord Theodore was already seated and waving out to him. Lord Percy eyed the seat opposite his friend. Both of them were in their late fifties and had descended from a long line of extremely wealthy aristocrats. They had been together at school as well as college.

'Good evening, Percy,' said Lord Theodore amiably and rose to shake hands with his friend. They had barely settled down when a butler came to them and bowed low.

'Get me a stiff eighteen-year-old Glenlivet on the rocks. How about you, Theo? Same for Lord Theodore as well, Manfred, thank you,' said Lord Percival. The butler bowed once more and waded away through the carpet.

'Well, Theo, that was a close call, wasn't it? You got lucky this time.'

Lord Theodore grinned at his friend.

'Have you got it with you? It's time to cough it up, old friend.'

'Always impatient! You haven't changed a bit since we were boys. All right, don't lose your cool. Here, take it. The combination code is 561413,' said Lord Percy, as he handed over the briefcase that he had been toting around.

Lord Theodore took the briefcase and quickly wrote down the combination in a small diary which he had produced from his pocket.

'I suppose I can trust that you have counted it yourself?'

Lord Percy looked up at Lord Theo with a pained expression. Theo hastily apologised and appeared embarrassed.

'Sorry, old chap. I have been having bad luck trusting people, even if they were family. It's become second nature to me to ask. Please forgive my ill-manners, dear boy.'

Just then the butler arrived with the drinks. Setting the glasses on the table, the butler departed to serve elsewhere, while the two reminisced over the final match.

'That was not the best of 100s by our boy, was it? Five missed opportunities! Four catches dropped, and one stumping attempt missed. You really were lucky this time, Theo. But a wager is a wager, and you won, fair and square.'

'Oh I don't know, Percy. It could have gone your way right at the start when our boy completely missed that in-swinger. God! That ball missed the stumps by only a millimetre, at the most,' said Theo with a shiver as he thought about the second delivery faced by Anthony Wells.

'I say, it's curious about those four Pakis, isn't it? The match-fixing scandal, I mean.'

'Hmmm. Do you have any idea who the master puppeteers were?'

Percy shook his head. He had been as puzzled as the rest of the nation about the whole episode.

'Anyway, it definitely did not affect our deal, did it?'

Both finished their drinks and, it being late, decided to head back to their homes. Outside, the drizzle had stopped and a cold westerly wind was now blowing gently, rustling the leaves. Lord Percival was the first to get into his car and depart. Lord Theodore waited outside the doorway of the club until the Bentley had turned a corner and was out of sight. He turned right and walked towards where his car was parked. This was one of the few times that Lord Theodore had decided to drive and had given his driver the evening off. The inconspicuous Skoda would not have caught any eye. It would appear to be one of thousands on the streets of London. Lord Theodore drove east, keeping well under the speed limit. He pondered over how it had all started. It was the semi-final match in which Anthony Wells had scored his second back-to-back century, this time against the West Indies, effectively knocking them out of the finals. After the match, while sitting at the club with Lord Percy, he had commented that Anthony Wells would score another century in the final. This had riled Lord Percy, as Anthony Wells belonged to Lord Theodore's County team. He had immediately laid a wager that if Wells scored fifty, he would pay Theo £500,000, and if he scored a century, he would pay him £1,000,000. Theo had immediately taken up the wager. He stood to lose a million pounds if Wells failed to score fifty. As he drove, Lord Theodore felt thoroughly embarrassed at having suckered his childhood friend. He recalled how nervous he had been when the final match had begun. He nearly had a heart attack when Wells was almost bowled on the very second ball of his innings. He had continued to be shaky until Wells had scored fifty, after which he had started breathing easily. God, what an awful lot of pressure he had been under!

Thirty minutes later, he parked in a narrow, secluded lane. He grabbed the briefcase from the back seat and kept it on his lap. He quickly opened it, using the combination provided by Lord Percival, and stared at the one million pounds which lay before him. From the glove compartment, he took out a blue plastic bag and began to count out £200,000, which he then transferred to the plastic bag. Locking the briefcase, he slid it under the passenger seat and again continued driving east.

Ten minutes later, he parked the car in a small lane near Canary Wharf Station and waited. It had started drizzling again. At midnight, a man dressed in a dark grey raincoat stood outside the telephone booth at the corner of the station. Lord Theodore took out his cell phone and dialled a number. The telephone in the booth rang three times, before it was picked up and immediately disconnected by the man in the raincoat. Lord Theodore walked up to the phone booth, just as the man got out.

'Walk with me,' commanded Lord Theodore. The man obliged. Although the streets were deserted, it would appear to anyone watching that the two men were returning home after a late evening in the office. Lord Theodore held out the plastic bag containing the £200,000, discreetly, and the man took it.

'Thank you,' he said, 'I hope it's all there.'

'You should know better than to ask such a question,' retorted Lord Theodore. The man nodded.

'Anything else, sir?' queried the man in grey.

'Yes, just one thing. I am sure you will distribute the cash evenly amongst all your players, but I would suggest that you do something about the four players who almost got me into a fix because of their greed. Why did they have to get into another deal when they already had a deal going on here?'

'That is not entirely correct, Lord Theodore,' said the man, uneasily.

'What do you mean?' demanded Lord Theodore. The man fell silent for a minute before answering.

'Well, sir, it is like this. As per our deal, Wells was to be allowed to make a century. I made sure that two of those four men, Rana and Mehboob, were rested when we were fielding and two other boys were sent in. It would have looked awfully suspicious if all the four had been rested. The missed stumping attempt when Wells was on sixteen, the first catch dropped when he was on thirty-three, and the third catch dropped when he was on sixty-seven were done by my men who were involved in our deal, but the second catch which was dropped on forty-eight and the fourth catch that was dropped when he was on ninety-nine were purely due to poor fielding in the outfield by Riazuddin and Omar.'

Lord Theodore stopped in his tracks suddenly and gasped at this shocking revelation.

The man continued nervously, 'Sir, the four players, who were accused earlier, were the only ones who refused to get involved in any form of match-fixing, including the deal that I offered them on your behalf. Goodnight, sir.' He said nervously and quickly walked away. Lord Theodore felt a spasm go through his right arm and his knees started shaking.

The man in grey continued to walk until he reached his car which was parked in a dark alleyway. He quickly got in, looked at himself in the mirror with relief, and grinned. He had pulled it off brilliantly! 'Thank God that he looked so similar to the senior Pakistani team manager,' thought Patel. He had been approached by Lord Theodore, while he was waiting outside the hotel rooms of the Pakistani cricket team for an autograph. Once Patel had understood that Lord Theodore had mistaken him for the senior team manager of the Pakistani team, he had brazenly taken up the role and demanded an upfront payment of £50,000 to lock the deal, as they sat in a coffee shop next to the hotel. The remaining £200,000 were to be paid up after completion of the deal at a place near Canary Wharf Station. Immediately after the deal was struck, he had decided to disappear into the heart of London forever with the £50,000, amongst the many Indians who had made England their home permanently. He would never have faced Lord Theodore again in his life. That is, until Anthony Wells had miraculously scored that century in the finals. Patel had seen the match on television and had wondered if he should go back and collect the remaining £200,000. His sharp, business-minded brain had produced a fantastic story for telling Lord Theodore, should he be asked about the four men accused of match-fixing. Well, he had no clue whether any of the Pakistani players were actually involved in any form of match-fixing; at least he had no hand in it. Fate had offered him a chance to make money, and he had taken it. After all, he was just a businessman.

11

Cowboys from the East

'WE DON'T SERVE injuns in here, chief,' growled the bartender at me, with an ominous scowl. My sun-bleached skin and tanned complexion had caused him to confuse me with the original inhabitants of this vast country.

Looking at the bartender through my exhaustion, I failed to see the three men who quietly stood up and got behind me. The next instant, they had picked me up and thrown me out through the bat-wing doors of the saloon, into the water-trough outside. They burst out laughing when they saw my discomposure. When I tried to get out of the trough, one of the men drew out his revolver and started shooting near my legs. They roared with laughter, yelling and shouting, in their drunken state. Hearing the commotion, a few people gathered on the dusty street, and some of the men from the saloon came out and watched the fun silently. Entertainment such as this was not uncommon here.

'C'mon, chief! Do a li'l war dance fer us gents out here,' yelled one of the brutes, while his friends guffawed loudly.

After a few minutes of this, I decided on another way to get out of the horse-trough. My grandpa had always said that attack was the best form of defence. I jumped out of the trough and launched a flying kick at the two men closest to me. This move took them by surprise, and I knocked two of them out cold, my fury giving me the strength. As the two men fell, I turned around just as a shot rang out and crippled the third man's right arm. He had been about to shoot me in the back. The crowd gasped as I stood frozen and looked around for my benefactor. There stood a giant of a man next to the saloon door, with his back resting against the wall, looking on nonchalantly, while blue smoke from the gun in his left hand curled in the air. The fun was over, so the small crowd, which had collected there, quickly walked away.

'You aw'right, son?' asked the tall middle-aged man in a quiet voice, as he put away his gun. I nodded and stood swaying, eyeing the two unconscious men at my feet, while the third held on to his injured hand, muttering curses through clenched teeth.

I was tired, dusty, and worn out. The vast Great Basin Desert had taken every ounce of my prowess to survive the crossing and enable me to arrive at the outskirts of Salt Lake City. It had taken me twenty-seven days to cross the expanse of the desert from Sacramento. Although I had taken Fremont's Route of 1845, I was new to the country and often misread the route on my crude, hand-drawn map. Just a few hours before reaching the saloon that afternoon, I had been shot at and chased by a group of rough-looking men until my horse had collapsed under me. I had managed to hold them off with my Sharps rifle for some time and had finally crept away through the trees, without realising that I had dropped my revolver. I was a lad of merely fifteen years of age, far away from the land I knew as home.

'Gid outta here an' take yore two sidekicks with yu. If I see yu first, I will shoot to kill,' warned the tall man, looking at the man whose hand he had shot. The bully whimpered and sat down on the ground next to his fallen comrades.

'Let's get yu fed an' mended, if yu have no objections,' said the tall man to me gently. I nodded once more and followed the man into a nearby abode whose dirt-streaked and pockmarked banner proclaimed it to be a restaurant. My dip in the horse-trough had gotten rid of most of the desert sand and street dust from my clothes and face. We went in, and he motioned me to take a chair in front of him. When the restaurant owner came up to us, he looked at me hesitantly but relaxed immediately, when he saw who I was with.

'Steak an' potatoes for both of us,' ordered the tall man.

'No steak for me. Just bread and potatoes or any other vegetables that you might have, sir,' I said, being a vegetarian. Both of them looked at me in amazement, not sure what to make of me. I had spoken with a slight British accent that I had acquired from my English teacher back home. When the amazed owner went to prepare our food, the tall man looked at me curiously.

'Le's get acquainted. I am Walter Severn, a rancher from near Fort Laramie, Nebraska. What's yore name, son?'

I had not spoken to anyone for those twenty-seven days when I was crossing the desert, so this was a welcome conversation.

'My name is Arjun. I am from India,' I said. He looked puzzled.

'Yu mean Indian Territory, near Arkansas?'

'No, sir. India, it's a country in Asia. I am sure you must have heard of it,' I said, correcting him. He looked at me in amazement and slapped his leg.

'Damn me! Is that true?' he exclaimed, astounded with my origins.

'Yes, sir,' I said. He looked at me with a hint of suspicion, which he shook off, unable to fathom if I was pulling his leg.

'Gawd! Yu are the first original Indian I have ever met, son. Never expected yu would look like this,' he blurted out and was immediately contrite, hoping I had not been offended. I smiled at his confusion and said it was all right.

'How in God's wide world did yu land up here, lad?' he asked eagerly.

'It's a long story, sir,' I replied tiredly.

'We have all the time in the world, son. It will be a while before the cook manages to find them vegetables fer yu. Shoot, I am all ears,' said Walter.

Tired as I was, I explained to him, 'I am the crown prince of the kingdom of Patwardh in the west-central part of India. It was somewhere around the peak of the 1857 Indian Rebellion that my grandfather, the King of Patwardh, was on his way to attend a meeting of kings and noblemen who were opposed to a new British law for Indians, which refused the right of ascendancy to their heirs, without their express approval. He was killed near the western border of the state of Hyderabad, before he could reach the meeting point.

'News of his death had been brought back by a monk who had passed through that area when he had come upon the site of the massacre. My father and a small army had gone to inspect the area for clues and to retrieve his body. He had been beheaded, and his headless body had been thrown into the forest along with his loyal troops, all lying dead. From all signs, it appeared that soldiers from the East India Company had been lying in wait and had ambushed my grandpa and his men. My father was crowned as the king soon after my grandpa's death, in June 1857. At that time, the British were greedily robbing India of every valuable, under the guise of the East India Company. My grandfather was one of many kings, who had refused to bow down to the British rule in India. It was in 1850, when my grandfather took a stand against having a representative of the East India Company permanently stationed in the courts of the kingdom that an open feud had begun between the company and us.

'My mother died the day I was born. Right from the beginning, I was very close to my grandpa, rather than my father. My memory of him is that of a gigantic man with a huge white bristling moustache and a flowing grey beard. He had a deep and opulent voice. As a toddler, I had seen him return from battlefields, bleeding and torn, but with never a tremor in his rumbling voice. From conversations amongst the palace servants, which I was privy to, he was rumoured to be indestructible. My father was not in his best books, having married the daughter of a noble man who was not trusted by my grandfather, within a year of my mother's death. Although he was always courteous with his daughter-in-law, my stepmother, he never forgave his son for going against his wishes. My father, although a very intelligent man, always avoided confrontations and seldom accompanied my grandpa during battles. He was a meek soul which made my grandpa furious with him. My stepmother and I rarely interacted, and there was nothing but taciturn respect for each other between us.

Under my grandpa's personal supervision, my training began extensively from the day I turned eight, which continued over the next six years. I became proficient in the arts of warfare, sciences, and languages. Surprisingly, there was one Englishman in our entire durbar. His name was Dr Andrew Taylor, who hailed from London and was also my tutor. He was the only Englishman whom my grandfather could tolerate. They would discuss poetry, politics, and policy. Before I turned fifteen, my reputation as a quick-witted and brave leader had already been established. The East India Company fearing that a young man with hot blood and fresh ideas could be a thorn in their side at a later date decided to abduct me so that the Kingdom of Patwardh would slowly succumb to their will, knowing that my father, the king, would not be keen on a confrontation. They had made several attempts, but I was always well guarded.

It was in January 1858, when I, along with my most trustworthy soldiers, was on a hunting expedition in the jungles south of the Kingdom of Kolhapur, which bordered our territory, that I was kidnapped. A traitor in our royal court must have given details of our hunt to the British. After a prolonged skirmish with the soldiers of the East India Company, I was overpowered and captured. To the east of my ancestral land, lay the state of Hyderabad, which was sympathetic to the British cause. This was where I was incarcerated for three months before being transported to the port city of Calcutta. I have no idea if any of my brave soldiers had survived the attack. I found myself at the bottom of a cargo hold on a ship bound for Shanghai, which reached there after twenty days, on my fifteenth birthday. After almost four months of waiting in Shanghai, I was taken on board another sailing ship which was headed for San Francisco. I was constantly guarded all this time, by five hefty soldiers of the East India Company.

While en route to San Francisco, on 1 October 1858, we ran into a gale. In the early morning of 2 October 1858, the ship ran aground and foundered. In the ensuing melee, I found myself in the rough seas and managed to hold onto a wooden beam that was adrift. I must have floated for several hours, and finally at day break, I was washed ashore. When I saw no other survivors, I took to my heels and ran into the hinterland, trying to put as much distance between me and anyone who might be following. By next morning, I found myself close to a massive house which was painted white. All around, grapes and oranges grew abundantly but in an organised manner. Hungry and tired, I decided to try knocking on the door of that beautiful house.

The house belonged to a gentleman called Mr Barton, who, when I related my story, sympathised with my plight and offered me accommodation in his home. He was a well-read man and was a grower of grapes and oranges in his acres of orchards which were situated in a valley called Napa. I learnt from him that I was now in the state of California, in the United States of America and Territories of the Union. I was an mystery to him right from day one. I would spend most of the day riding with Mr Barton through the orchards. In the evenings, I would read everything I could about the country that I was in. I spent several weeks there, until my restlessness was evident to him. One day, he asked me about it, and I confessed that I was keen to return to my homeland. We sat down in his well-stocked library and poured over a map of the United States and Territories of the Union. Over the course of the full day, we chalked out a route that I could safely follow. We had immediately decided against me going back to San Francisco, for we feared that agents of the East India Company would immediately identify me and either arrest me or even kill me. The best option was to head in the east-north-easterly direction, keeping well clear of all the slave-holding states in the south and then to get to New York, from where I could board a ship going to England and then onwards to India. I felt sure that the last place where the British would look for me was England. He marked this route on a rough sketch of the country from coast to coast, marking places where I could rest safely on the way to New York. I insisted on including two towns which I was curious to visit. I had always thought that Delhi was a place only in India. The plan had appeared feasible and clever. Reality was a different matter altogether, as I found out later.

'The next day, he gave me a horse, saddle, a canteen of water, a bedroll, and a leather saddle bag to hold some dried fruits, biscuits, and coffee, a six-shot Colt 1851 Root revolver with a 0.31 calibre and a single shot Sharps 1853 carbine with a 0.52 calibre. The map with my route was tucked into my shirt pocket. Just after we shook hands and bid each other farewell, he handed me a small leather sack which contained gold coins worth 200 dollars. He insisted that I keep it when I refused such gratitude. I rode away from the house, while the old man watched from the front porch, with tears in his eyes. In the short time that I had spent with him, he had come to look upon me as his son, while he reminded me of a benevolent image of my grandfather. I then made the 520-mile journey across the Great Basin Desert using Fremont's route of 1845, surviving on certain species of cactus, which Mr Barton had told me a great deal about, beans, and some biscuits.'

Walter looked at me in amazement and whistled when I ended my story.

'Yu crossed the Great Basin on yore own? That must have been some ordeal, son!'

'I had no other choice, sir.'

He pondered over the story that I had told him. Just then, the cook brought us our food, Walter's plate with his steak and potatoes, and mine with some bread and a bowl of stewed potatoes, cabbage, carrots, and some strange-looking roots. We dug into our food, and for the next half-hour, there was only the sound of forks and knives striking our plates.

'So what's yore next plan, son?' asked Walter, sitting back after he had finished his food, as he rolled a cigarette. I was sure that this man could be trusted, so I opened the map that I had been carrying with me and showed it to him. He looked at the crumpled piece of paper and read it out.

'Hmmm . . . Bridger's Pass at the Utah-Nebraska border . . . south of the Black Hills . . . good . . . Fort

Laramie . . . past Scott's Bluff . . . then east to cross the Missouri River at Sargents Bluff where the three states of Nebraska, Iowa, and Minnesota meet . . . Fort Dodge in Iowa . . . ha, Delhi in Iowa, near river Maquoketa . . . Gatena . . . Chicago . . . Toledo . . . Cleveland . . . Dunkirk . . . Rochester . . . Syracuse . . . Binghamton . . . hello, Delhi in New York state . . . Catskill . . . and then New York City.'

Walter looked up at me with pity.

'Son, do yu know how difficult this entire journey is going to be? It's not jus' about the huge distance or the harsh climate through those mountain passes that I am talkin' about. There is the danger of running into Indians. And I don't mean yore type of Indians. These are ferocious tribes known as the Apaches, Sioux, and the Cheyenne, who will likely skin yu or scalp you alive, jus' because they are on the warpath with the white men.'

I nodded. When I was in Mr Barton's library, I had read up about the various tribes of indigenous people who, in my opinion, were the real owners of this land. In fact, during some of our discussions, Mr Barton and I had argued whether the problems faced in India were not similar to those faced by the tribes of the Red Indians, as they had come to be known, thanks to Columbus.

'I don't have a choice, sir, do I?' I replied quietly. Walter sat in deep thought while he smoked. After sometime, he appeared to come to a decision.

'Aw'right, son. I believe yu deserve a chance to succeed after all that yu have been through,' he paused, looking at me closely, and continued, 'I will be heading back to my ranch near Fort Laramie tomorrow. It's on yore route and jus' north-east of Scott's Bluff. Yu are welcome to join me an' my boys on the way back. How does that sound to yu?'

I was so pleased with the thought of some company that I jumped to my feet and shook his hand eagerly, thanking him for his kindness. He looked extremely embarrassed and frowned good naturedly.

I still had the $200 in gold coins that Mr Barton had given me, so I told Walter that I would pay for my upkeep. He smiled at this and merely nodded.

That night, I had a blissful sleep for the first time in the last three weeks and that too on a comfortable bed in my hotel room. Walter had the adjoining room and had argued with the landlord, until he had reluctantly let me have a room. It seemed to me that there were some people even in the non-slave states or Free states as they were known, with prejudices against the colour of a man's skin.

Early next day, when I went down for a breakfast of beans and bread, four other men had joined Walter. He introduced me to them as Slim, Bill, Mac, and Jim. Each of them shook my hand warmly, with a friendly smile. Walter must have told them my story, I guessed. During breakfast, Walter presented me with a Colt Root revolver 1851, with a 0.28 calibre and sufficient cartridges. It was a six-shot, same as my earlier gun but with a smaller calibre.

Immediately after breakfast, we mounted our steeds and were on the trail to Fort Bridger. We stopped overnight near the Bear River and went across the next day, reaching Fort Bridger late that night. The next day, we rode on till we reached Bitter Creek and then camped for the night there. We had planned to cross Bridger's Pass the following day, starting early, as the cold mountain winds were supposed to be terrible and could kill, if exposed to it for a long period. The four cowhands with Walter treated me like one of them, and I had no cause for any complaint. We had seen few people on the trail since leaving Fort Bridger. We had come across a cavalry guarding a stagecoach, a group of miners, and once, even passed a band of Cherokee Indians, who ignored us completely much to my disappointment. The cowhands laughed at me when I suggested that we should go and talk to them. Fortunately, we made it across safely and entered the state of Nebraska.

I had been keeping track of our journey using my hand-drawn map, ticking the places and landmarks marked on it, as we passed them. After the tiring climb and the precarious descent through Bridger's Pass, we rested again and camped at the southern part of the North Fork Platte River. The six of us had a discussion on the next phase of our journey, which was supposed to be the most crucial and dangerous. Walter warned us that we would be riding hard, until we crossed over the southern part of the Black Hills and reached Pole Creek, where we would rest for the night. From that moment on, two of us took turns at keeping a sentry watch. Nothing worthwhile happened in the night, except for a coyote that came close to our camp, and we almost shot him dead. Next morning, we hit the trail hard and nudged our mounts to move faster. As we closed in on the Black Hills, the air was filled with the smell of ponderosa pine trees. My companions were extremely alert; their hands always close to the guns at their hips, and we rarely spoke to each other. I sensed the danger around us, the air pregnant with the sense of anticipation of an attack by the Sioux, who were one of the most notorious of the tribes in these parts. We had now passed three tributaries of the Laramie River and had planned to rest only when we had reached Horse Creek, which lay in the southern part of the Black Hills. Walter had told me that from Pole Creek to his ranch would take us about five hours. Just as we climbed up a butte to cross the Black Hills, we ran into trouble.

A shot rang out and downed the cowhand called Slim, who was riding ahead with Bill. We immediately jumped off our horses and dived for whatever cover we could find, as more shots followed the first. We lay quietly in the brush, without moving.

'Keep extremely still, son,' whispered Walter, the worry in his voice clearly apparent. He had been riding with me throughout the journey during which he had taught me a lot about the country.

I kept as still as I could. It is actually a fact that whenever you are told to be quiet and still in such situations, the urge to scratch an urgent itch or to sneeze or cough is the strongest. The same thing was happening to me, but I controlled it with a superhuman effort. We must have waited in complete silence for about half an hour, wondering if Slim was alive. He too had disappeared in the sagebrush. Walter finally took off his hat and held it in the air at the end of a stick. There were no shots fired. We continued waiting for another tense hour, but there was no attack. Finally, Walter got to his feet and signalled us with a low whistle. The moment we stood up, the Sioux, who had been steadily crawling through the thick brush, attacked us with horrible shrieks. I was dumbfounded and stood rooted to the spot. The others were also taken by surprise, but after a bare moment of hesitation, they drew their guns and fired into the midst of the attackers. Within a few ticks, six of the Sioux lay dead at our feet, while the others disappeared as quickly as they had attacked. I realised that I had still got my revolver in its holster, without even touching it, so fast was the strike. In the aftermath, I snatched out my gun and looked around frantically for a target.

'Take it easy, son. Don't yu fret no more. Yu will git yore chance soon enough. We are used to these kind o' methods,' said the cowhand known as Mac, soothingly.

We quickly went around and checked on Slim, who lay bleeding behind a tiny rock. He had been shot through his thigh, but the wound was a clean one, the bullet having passed through and through. Mac and Walter quickly fashioned a tourniquet and bound his injury tightly. Bill and Jim stood guard around us, while I kept my revolver in my hand. Once Slim was proclaimed ready and fit to travel,

Bill and Jim were about to go and get hold of our horses which had run away during the skirmish, when the second wave of attack took place. This time I used my gun and shot at a couple of the attackers. The only problem was there were too many of them, and so, after an hour of fighting; we succumbed to the overwhelming numbers of the Sioux.

They bound us up tightly, and having collected our weapons, they made us walk in a straight file in a northerly direction. Six hours later, we reached a valley in the Black Hills which was naturally protected by the curvature of the hill range. I saw that several fires had been lit and there was a lot of activity in the settlement of tepees. We were immediately thrown into a dark cavern, whose mouth was covered with buffalo hide. Outside, there was wailing and ululating going on for the Sioux braves whom we had killed. Once we were alone, Walter immediately made sure that all of us were accounted for and confirmed that none of us were badly injured. In the dim light, he looked extremely grave and grim. It was a tight spot that we were in. The Sioux always tried to keep their prisoners intact so that the torture could be long and severe.

That night, we were fed with a strange smelling gruel and some kind of bread. Shortly after our meal, their chief came in with four of his braves, while two stood guard outside. One of the braves was carrying a flaming torch in his hand. The chief looked at us slowly and carefully. When his eyes reached me, he looked surprised and grunted. He leaned down and peered at me carefully, while I kept a brave face and looked at him straight in the eye. He spied the gold chain with its pendant which I had been wearing ever since I was eight years old. With a quick snatch, he ripped of the chain and took a close look at the pendant and gasped. It was made of solid gold and carved with our royal crest and coat of arms. A lion with his mouth wide open showing huge fangs, the eyes embedded with two tiny red rubies and beneath one of the front paws was a jackal being crushed, while under the other was a bear. The chief exclaimed, and his darting eyes showed a curious fear. He immediately threw the chain and the pendant at me and said something to his braves. Two of them released our bonds, and the chief motioned us to follow him outside.

'Stay behind me,' whispered Walter to me. We realised that something had upset the Sioux chief and we were either going to be executed immediately or tortured. I did as I was told, while Slim and Bill flanked me on both sides and Jim and Mac brought up the rear. The chief said something to the Sioux who had gathered around. They immediately fell back. He then said something to a few of his braves who immediately ran away to do his bidding. I put my chain and pendant around my neck again, as the Sioux gathered around, gazing at me curiously. Soon, we heard horses coming our way and found that they were our steeds, brought back by the Sioux braves. The chief then came towards us. He motioned Walter to stand aside, who reluctantly moved to one side, his body tensed and ready to react if any threatening move was made towards me. My heart thudded in anticipation as the chief came up to me. Speaking something in Sioux, he put his right hand on his heart and then on my heart. He stopped abruptly, and with his hands, he motioned us to go away. An astonished Walter and his men could not believe what they were witnessing. We immediately ran to our horses and found our guns and belongings tied to the saddles. As Walter and the cowhands mounted their horses with a new-found urgency, I lagged behind and impulsively went up to the chief. He looked down at me from his great height, impassively. Using the Sanskrit language of ancient India, I said that I came in peace and was going in peace, putting my right hand on my heart and then on his. The chief looked at me curiously and nodded gravely, as if he understood every word of what I had just said! Strangely, at that moment, I wondered what, if anything, in this world would have made him smile. I turned and immediately mounted my horse. Within minutes, we were thundering down south, as far away as we could get from that place.

My mind was full of questions. I pondered over the reaction of the Sioux chief and his braves when they had seen my pendant. That something about the pendant had scared them, I was sure. But what? And why? We crossed over the Laramie River and finally reached Horse Creek, exactly where we had been ambushed. Our horses were tired, and the smell of water drew them to the creek. It was still five hours of riding to Walter's ranch which he told me was located north of Chunney Rock. We got off our mounts to rest them, as well as to give ourselves a break. It was unlikely that the Sioux would attack us again, especially after their chief had just liberated us. It was early morning, and we were tired after the all night ride. We first sat down and had some breakfast and coffee.

'What do you think happened back there, sir?' I asked Walter. He took a deep pull from his coffee mug and peered into the embers of the fire under the coffee pot. Walter asked me if he could take a look at my pendant, so I handed it over to him. The others came forward to take a closer look. I had kept it hidden in my underclothing, just before I had been taken captive by the East India Company and had only started wearing it again, when we had started from Salt Lake City.

'Dang me if that warn't the strangest thing ever to happen to me!' exclaimed Jim. The other three agreed with him.

'I can think of only two possibilities,' said Walter thoughtfully and paused, turning the pendant in his hand and scrutinising the engraving. 'First, the engraving on the pendant probably shows a Sioux sign for trouble. Probably their totem symbol is depicted as being mauled by the Lion. The second possibility is that the chief recognised the symbols as those of a friendly tribe and so he let us go free.'

'Hell, Walt! I don't care why the darned injuns let us go free, but we must thank this young lad here, without whose pendant we would all be dead or wishing we were dead,' exclaimed Mac.

The four cowhands started a good-natured banter over our miraculous escape from the clutches of the Sioux, which made us all light-hearted and heady. After a quick meal of the last of our rations, we decided to rest for a while before resuming the last stage of our journey. Well, it was the last stage for them, but I still had to cover two-thirds of my journey to New York, not to mention getting back to India. We still maintained our alertness, with two of us taking up guard duties every two hours. Just after noon, we got back on our horses and proceeded towards Walter's ranch, much refreshed by the break.

We reached the ranch that same evening, just as the sun was setting, and were hailed by a shout from the ranch house, which immediately caused several cowhands to pour out from an extension of the house. It was the most curious structure that I had ever seen, except for the tepees of the Sioux. Built partly from wood and partly from stone, it appeared very cosy from the distance. The man hailing us from the veranda in front of the house was the foreman, who stood up with a shotgun in his hands. The men from the ranch whooped loudly and ran forward to meet us.

'Aw'right, boys! The boss is back, so y'all will git yore money tomorrow,' said the foreman to the men, with a smile on his face. We dismounted and entered the ranch, while Bill, Jim, Mac, and Slim made for the bunkhouse, where they joined the other cowhands.

'Dudley, good to see yu agin,' said Walter, shaking hands with the foreman. 'This lad here is Arjun, whom I met in Salt Lake City.'

Dudley came forward and shook hands with me and frowned. I was a little discomforted by the frown, but his next words eased the tension.

'Sorry, lad but you reminded me powerfully o' someone,' said Dudley and continued looking at me strangely. Later, I found out that he was a southerner but had chosen to come up north and remain here.

'Let's go inside an' wash up, kid,' said Walter. The interior of the ranch house was lit with lanterns and candles. It had been well decorated, but there was an aura of melancholy in the faded curtains and dilapidated furniture which had once seen better days and upkeep.

'This 'ere was all done by my wife. She died seven years ago an' since then I didn't have the heart to keep the place as well as she had,' explained Walter, clearly knowing what was in my mind. He showed me where to clean up, and after an hour, we sat down in the drawing room. The cook, who had a peg leg, came out with some food. Between bites, Walter then told Dudley the whole story, starting with his own successful cattle run to Salt Lake City, how he had met me, and ending at our release from the Sioux. Dudley exclaimed loudly and looked at me with amazement in the candle light. Walter looked at him sharply while I gazed at Dudley wondering what he had in his mind.

'What's wrong, Dud?' asked a puzzled Walter.

'Holy cow! Mind showing me that pendant, son?' said Dudley, his excitement very evident. I removed the pendant and chain from around my neck and handed it over to Dudley. Dudley almost snatched it from my hand, and holding it up to the light, he whooped with delight.

'Mind explaining the rejoicing?' said Walter, sarcastically. He later told me that Dudley was a man who never showed his emotions openly and so he had been surprised at the way Dudley had behaved.

'No. No . . . no . . . no. This, yu have to wait and see fer yoreself,' said Dudley, shaking his head in amazement.

Walter grunted with exasperation but did not say anything. Dudley handed me my chain and pendant, with a delighted grin on his large face, and I immediately put it back around my neck. He turned to Walter and said, 'Boss, yu have bin away for three weeks. The day y'all left for Salt Lake City, we found a stranger on our way back from Fort Laramie near the North Fork Butte. He was badly injured, but we fixed him up good and brought him here. He has bin stayin' with us since an' helping out with things. He should be here any minute, so yu can see him fer yoreself.'

We finished our dinner and had just sat down, when a horse neighed outside, and we heard the trot of his treads. Curiosity was killing me and Walter too, so we stood up and made for the door. In the darkness outside, we saw the silhouette of tall, well-built man who was tying up his horse to the railing of the veranda. He looked up immediately when he heard us, and my heart almost stopped.

'Hello, Mr Dudley. Looks like you have visitors,' said the man in a deep voice with a strange but familiar accent. I had seen and heard this man before. There could be no two men exactly similar. The shock of his sight had frozen my tongue and body. The man walked up the stairs and stopped midway, also frozen with shock when he saw me. With a cry of delight, I threw myself at the man who still looked at me with disbelief. Then he broke down completely and gave me a bear hug so tightly that I could barely breath.

'How in all that is holy did you get here, Arjun?' he asked, between tears of joy. Walter had meanwhile been astounded by all this activity. My yell of delight had also brought all the cowhands running out from the bunkhouse, their guns drawn and ready for trouble. They stopped when they saw the scene I was creating.

'Walt, this here is the guy I told y'all about. He has the same pendant around his neck as this young lad,' explained Dudley excitedly.

After a while, we went back into the ranch house, followed by all the cowhands, whom Walter had asked to join us.

'Sir, this is my grandfather, the King of Patwardh. If you recollect, I had mentioned him to you when we first met in Salt Lake City,' I told Walter, who shook his head in amazement. The cowhands, who had heard the entire story from Jim, Mac, Bill, and Slim, whooped and yelled with delight. Then it was time for both of us to explain how we came into our situation. My grandfather uttered profanities when he heard of the deception with which I had been captured by the soldiers of the East India Company. After I had finished my story, he stood up and took Walter's hand in both of his own and thanked him profusely, tears streaming down from his eyes. Walter looked extremely uncomfortable and embarrassed but managed to keep his discomfiture to himself.

'I believe in miracles, but this is one outa the blue,' exclaimed Walter, while the others whistled in agreement.

'Would yu mind telling us how yu come to be here, seh? From what this young lad told me, yu were killed in India,' asked Walter, politely. He was not sure how to talk to a king.

'Well, Mr Walter, if you will bear with me, I will tell you what happened and how. I was waylaid when I was on the route from Patwardh to a place, the name of which I am still under oath not to reveal, where a group of like-minded Indian noblemen and kings were to hold a meeting to decide our action against the East India Company. They had introduced the Doctrine of Lapse, by which, no nobleman or king could be replaced with his own direct descendant, as has been our tradition in India. The East India Company wanted to appoint their own candidate, who would be loyal to them and them alone. It was this law which we were hoping to bring down with negotiations, keeping the option of armed conflict open. As I was the leader of this group, the East India Company wanted me out of the way, and so with the help of a traitor in my court, they laid a trap and captured me and my men after a prolonged and bloody fight. Then they took my clothes, sword, and my horse. However, my royal pendant had fallen during the skirmish, so they could not find it. Luckily, I found it lying in the grass where they had trussed me up. They searched around and found one of my dead soldiers, who had exactly my build, and dressed him up in my clothes. He was then beheaded. None of my soldiers survived. I was then taken by ship to Shanghai and then after some time, to San Francisco. The same night that we reached San Francisco, I managed to overpower and kill all my guards. I stole whatever I could from them. I remained there for a few weeks, learning about where I was, until I had decided on a plan of action which would take me to New York and then to India via England. After stealing a horse, I set off across the desert, bypassed all the settlements and towns, and got into countless fights with the Apaches, Cheyenne, and the Sioux. I must have made some kind of an impression on them, as by the time I reached the place called Black Hills, the Sioux there meekly accepted my presence and even fed me for a few days that I stayed with them. Then one night, we got into a fight with another tribe of Indians. During the fight, I was badly wounded and was luckily washed away into the North Fork Platte River. I was picked up from the shores, close to Fort Laramie, by Mr Dudley, where I had been lying unconscious for god knows how long,' said the king.

The cowhands murmured and exclaimed at the fantastic stories they were hearing, while Walter and Dudley looked on in fascination. I sat close to my grandpa, my mind completely muddled with the events when Walter spoke up.

'That was an amazing feat of daring, seh. To single-handedly gain the respect of any of the injuns is one of the highest achievements in this country. I would be honoured if yu and Arjun will agree to stay here for as long as yu want,' said Walter, generously. The king bowed his head in acceptance of Walter's offer.

'I thank you for your kind offer, Mr Walter, but hope that you will allow me and my grandson to leave in a week from now,' said my grandpa. I was startled.

'Seh? One week? I was hoping that yu would stay with us permanently. Cowboys from the East is what you will be known as from now on,' replied Walter with grin, while the others whooped with delight at the new name for us. The king looked at him with a smile.

'There is some unfinished business which I and young Arjun have to attend back in India. We have to make the traitor, who has dethroned me and dared to put Arjun, the crown prince, in danger of losing his life, pay with his own life,' said the king softly, but with an underlying menace which chilled the blood of the gathered men.

'But, grandpa, it will be impossible to find out who the traitor is!' I burst out, though I was eager to go home.

'No disrespect intended, seh, but Arjun may be right,' said Walter while Dudley nodded in agreement. The king smiled at us, with a curious mixture of embarrassment and sadness in his eyes.

'Before I killed my guards in San Francisco, I tortured the captain of the guards until he told me that the only thing he remembered about the traitor was a gold chain around his neck with a pendant depicting a lion with his mouth wide open showing huge fangs, the eyes embedded with two tiny red rubies, and a jackal being crushed beneath one of the front paws and a bear under the other. At first, my first suspicion was on young Arjun, as he alone had the guts to carry out such a daring plan. Sorry, I suspected you, Arjun, but it was only when I saw you here that I realised who the real traitor was. So I have to go back and kill the coward who dared to do away with his own father and then put his own son in harm's way so that he and his evil wife could take over my kingdom,' said the king softly, while we all stared at him in disbelief, completely dazed.